Praise for
Joint Custody

"Lauren Baratz-Logsted and her daughter, Jackie Logsted, have written a funny, wise, and sparkling romp. Gatz is a dog on a mission. Determined to keep his owners together by any means necessary, he takes matters into his own paws and rewrites a love story destined for disaster. A delight from my new favorite mother-daughter writing team."

—Adriana Trigiani, *New York Times* bestselling author of *Tony's Wife*

"I admit I am a sucker for stories about four-footed friends and for mother-daughter writing teams like the Logsteds. And the charm here is the narration by a wise-in-love dog. . . . A perfect romp to brighten your winter!"

—Caroline Leavitt, *New York Times* bestselling author of *With or Without You*

"The authors of *Joint Custody* take the reader on a delightful adventure, led by a determined, cheeky, endearing narrator named Gatz, a border collie on a mission to reunite his owners. Our hero may miss a few key signs along the way, but he shares his growing understanding of happiness, true love, friendship, and happy endings. Highly entertaining!"

—Amy Poeppel, author of *Musical Chairs* and *Limelight*

"A laugh-out-loud rom-com set in New York City's publishing world. . . . This touching, hilarious outing is worthy of two paws up."

—*Publishers Weekly* (starred review)

Titles by Lauren Baratz-Logsted and Jackie Logsted

Joint Custody
The Great Gatz

The Great Gatz

Lauren Baratz-Logsted

and

Jackie Logsted

JOVE
New York

A JOVE BOOK
Published by Berkley
An imprint of Penguin Random House LLC
penguinrandomhouse.com

Library of Congress Cataloging-in-Publication Data

Names: Baratz-Logsted, Lauren, author. | Logsted, Jackie, author.
Title: The great Gatz / Lauren Baratz-Logsted and Jackie Logsted.
Description: First edition. | New York: Jove, 2021.
Identifiers: LCCN 2021000426 (print) | LCCN 2021000427 (ebook) |
ISBN 9780593199602 (trade paperback) | ISBN 9780593199619 (ebook)
Subjects: GSAFD: Humorous fiction. | Love stories.
Classification: LCC PS3602.A754 G74 2021 (print) | LCC PS3602.A754 (ebook) |
DDC 813/.6—dc23
LC record available at https://lccn.loc.gov/2021000426
LC ebook record available at https://lccn.loc.gov/2021000427

First Edition: December 2021

Printed in the United States of America
1st Printing

Book design by Nancy Resnick
Title page image by Evgeniya Chertova / Shutterstock

For Pamela Harty, who makes dreams come true

The Great Gatsby

Flash forward to five months later

Red alert. RED ALERT! Douche move! DOUCHE MOVE!

I hurled myself at him and, with all the strength my little body possessed, knocked him to the floor.

He looked up at me, stunned, as I perched on his chest.

Yup. At some point down the road, someone is going to do something so douchey, I'm going to have to resort to *that*.

Prologue

A famous Russian writer once said that "happy families are all alike; every unhappy family is unhappy in its own way." Well, I don't know what the Russian word is for "bollocks." But since The Woman is English, I'm well versed in what the English word is, and it's: bollocks.

Just as the Jane Austen line—"It is a truth universally acknowledged, that a single man in possession of a good fortune must be in want of a wife"—is not universal at all and is only true of the specific world Austen created, the same is true of Leo Tolstoy's dis on happy families. It is true in his world. But in *the* world, the one I inhabit, happy families are not all alike. Indeed, just like unhappy families, they are infinite in their variety.

I know this for a fact because I happen to come from a happy family; two, actually—the one I inhabit with The Man (who, OK, isn't always a bundle of joy and occasionally suffers from depression, but we are happy together) and the one I inhabit with The Woman and New Man.

But just because it's a happy world we've made for ourselves, it doesn't mean we're a bunch of giddily mindless twits. It doesn't mean we don't have our share of troubles, conflicts, and heartaches.

Yeah, about those . . .

But maybe I should back up for a minute. If this is the first time for a reader encountering me, that reader would be justified in asking: Who's telling this story? Who's quoting Tolstoy and Austen at the reader right off the bat?

The answer: me, Gatz. A dog. Black-and-white. Border collie. Lean at twenty-two pounds, but filled with love.

Now, here's where some might begin to object: The *dog* is telling the story? To which I would point out that all good narratives require the willing suspension of disbelief. So I would heartily encourage all who enter here to just be willing and suspend.

Having introduced myself, I'm going to further take this opportunity to bring everyone up to speed.

Once upon a time, I was rescued from a shelter by The Man, a thirtysomething schlub with an apartment in Brooklyn and a career as a literary novelist. On the day he rescued me, while walking home, we encountered The Woman: British, Black, and Beautiful, making her a trifecta in the B department. She was an editor in the city. As far as I was concerned, it was love for all of us at first sight, and, indeed, love and cohabitation soon followed. That state of bliss lasted for a while, but over time their differences got the best of them—he's an introvert; she's an extrovert; they were oil-and-watering each other—and she moved out.

There ensued a period in which I did everything in my doggy power, including a suicidal run-in with a box of Valentine's Day chocolates, to bring them back together. But all my efforts were to no avail once The Woman met New Man, a bestselling novelist and a dead ringer for Henry Golding. How could The Man, how could *any* man, compete with that? Not to mention, New Man was an extrovert too, who loved doing all the things The Man hated to do, so they had the stuff-in-common thing going for them as a couple too. Feh.

I wanted to hate the guy—for a long time I *did* hate the guy—and I certainly let him know it. But after a long journey of pushing him away and a failed reconciliation between The Man and The Woman, I had an epiphany, if you will: when you love someone, you should want what's best for them, not what's best for them in relation to you.

Cliché it may be, but I read the writing on the wall, and that writing told me that New Man was right for The Woman in ways that The Man never had been and never could be, not without at least one person winding up miserable. The Man and The Woman had come together over their shared love of me. The Woman and New Man, however? They fell in love with each other.

So, here's where we left off the last time. It was August. The Woman and New Man had recently become engaged and were in the audience at an author event at the 92nd Street Y. On the panel were The Man and one other person, one of The Woman's authors, whom I'd previously thought of simply that way. But a light bulb went on over my head when I noticed that the author, looking cute in her braids, was a female version of The Man, right down to her backward Mets baseball cap and her clear antipathy for anything social. Could this person actually be New Woman? Could these two find love in the same way The Woman and New Man had? Could there be romantic hope for The Man yet?

I think we're all on the same page now.

Now that that's been established, we can turn the page together . . .

Chapter One

September

Most people reckon the new year begins on January 1, but I favor September. Maybe it's the school-year thing. Sure, I've never been to school myself, not even obedience school—why would I ever need such a thing?—but it is when all the kids traditionally go back. It's also the month of Rosh Hashanah, the Jewish New Year, and while The Man is currently nonpracticing, I like to keep abreast of all the major holidays. You never know what could happen; you never know when things might suddenly change; you never know when good ol' Gatz might be called upon to don a yarmulke. I bet I'd wear one with élan.

So, September: a time for new beginnings, a season of renewal, change in the air.

What better time for The Woman to finally move in with New Man?

By this point, they'd been engaged for several weeks already. And while some might wonder why they didn't move in together immediately upon their engagement, I figured the delay had to do with deciding what to do about her own place, which her parents actually owned, or maybe she didn't want to rush everything like she'd done when she first met The Man; you know, maybe she was doing the live-and-learn thing.

Anyway, Moving Day had arrived!

I confess to being a bit anxious about it myself. Not everyone realizes this, but moving from one domicile to another is a top ten cause for anxiety when it comes to humans. And while I try to be as Zen as possible about most things, I had my concerns.

As anxiety-inducing as it can be to move in general, it's got to be exponentially more so when you're moving into someone else's space. If the place is new for everyone, then it's equally new for everyone. But if one of the people already lives there, it's not equal: it's *their space*! Similarly, if you're the person whose space it already is, then when someone else moves into it—bringing along her dog, say—it wouldn't be surprising if you experienced some sense of invasion, like: *Hey, you're in* my space*!*

So yeah, I had my anxieties about it. And on some level, I must have assumed that they wouldn't want me around on Moving Day, even though it occurred on the weekend, my normal time to be with The Woman, that and most holidays as per her joint-custody agreement with The Man. I figured that it might be a bit of a nuisance having a dog underfoot when you're trying to figure out if the credenza should stay where it's always been or if maybe it would work better against another wall.

New Man, however, was having none of it.

"Of course Gatz will be with us on Moving Day," he said, flashing his beautiful, charming, sweet smile at The Woman when she suggested that maybe it would be more convenient if she and The Man flipped their days with me that week. "Who else is going to tell me where to put my credenza?"

This guy, man. He was growing on me by the second.

New Man lives in the penthouse of a high-rise—actually has a special key to use in the elevator—and it's already decorated to perfection. With the exception of the mirrored bathroom floor—which I happen to like, but that I get others might find tacky—everything is perfectly appointed, every design decision exuding understated elegance. Because when you have a view like New

Man's, a floor-to-ceiling giant pane of glass spanning one entire wall and offering a view of the city that I doubt could be rivaled anywhere else *in* the city, you don't need to gild the lily with a whole bunch of tacky gold this and tacky gold that.

Not that any of The Woman's possessions are tacky. She herself is taste personified, which probably should've given me pause in her previous relationship with The Man, who is anything but. I guess it never had, though, until they broke up, because I happen to love the schlub myself, just as he is.

So, no, I hadn't worried that her things would clash with New Man's, but I had worried about the logistics of things. When she'd moved in with The Man, he'd first made space in the closet, made space in the bathroom, and, most important of all, made space on his bookshelves. The Man, though, wasn't much of a nester. Except for his collection of books and a few select articles of clothing, he wasn't married to any material objects. It didn't matter. But all the items in New Man's space were so well chosen, so well placed, how could he not object to our bringing along our own stuff and messing with his fêng shui?

The Woman and I took the elevator up to the penthouse apartment using her own new special key, The Woman carrying a box in her arms and me carrying some toys in my jaws. She grinned down at me and I looked up at her (my eyes glistening at her beauty, I'm sure).

"Are you ready, Gatz?" she asked me.

That was The Woman all over. She always thought of me. She always thought of us all.

I dropped my toys and barked my approval.

When we arrived, me trotting in more anxious still, it soon became apparent that New Man hadn't done anything in advance of our coming.

Did he not know what day it was?

"I kept thinking I should be doing something," he said, running a hand through his gloriously thick black hair. "I should be making room: clearing a shelf in the bookcase, adding a hook for your coffee mug next to mine even though I don't hang my mugs on hooks, or moving all my clothes over to one side of the closet. But then I thought: Why do that?"

Because it's the polite thing to do?

"That would be going about it all wrong."

Would it be?

And may I add here that The Woman and I shared a perplexed look at this turn of events. Perhaps she too had been experiencing some advance anxiety over an anticipated transitional awkwardness?

"From the looks on your faces," New Man said, "I can tell I'm expressing myself poorly."

Clearly.

And he calls himself a writer. Ha!

"If I'd done that," New Man said, trying again, "then you'd always feel—both you and Gatz—like 'OK, then, this is my small space here, my small place in the closet, et cetera, within his much larger space.' Do you see how wrong that would be?"

I was beginning to. From the growing curiosity in her eyes, I could tell The Woman was beginning to see it too.

"I want it all, everything here and every inch of it," New Man said, spreading his arms wide, "to be *our* space—all three of ours, whenever Gatz is here."

"Meaning . . . ?" The Woman said.

"Put your stuff wherever you want it, move anything you want to move, get rid of anything you hate. Like, for example, the credenza. Gatz, what do you think? Is it right where it is? Should we move it, or even get rid of it entirely?"

I tilted my head to one side to better regard the piece of furniture in question. Eh, I had no quarrel with the credenza.

While I was doing that, The Woman closed the space between

her and New Man, landing a passionate kiss on his lips. It went on for a really long time, their arms wrapping around each other, their bodies pressed so tightly together that I began to wonder if this might turn out to be one of those times where they just headed off to the bedroom and the mattress would begin to shake. When the two pulled away, a surprised blush escaped across his face. "What was that for?"

"For being you." She smiled, holding him close in her arms. "For wanting it all to be ours. And for making me feel instantly like it all is."

I thumped my tail enthusiastically and let out a happy bark so they'd both know that I felt the same.

Immediately, all my anxiety left me. What had I been so worried about?

That's the funny thing I've learned about anxiety, worry, and a whole host of negative emotions: Unless feeling it is going to make you do something to change your behavior in a positive way, what good does it do? What purpose does it serve? Nothing whatsoever, except to make the person experiencing it feel bad. And, worst of all, lots of times you feel these things in advance, and then the thing you were advance-anxious about never comes to pass, and all your anxiety is for naught. Yeah, I know all this, on an intellectual level. But on an emotional level? In the moment, like a lot of people, I do tend to forget.

"So," New Man said, "what do you want to change first?"

"Nothing," The Woman said, laughing. I guess all the anxiety had left her too. "We can do whatever needs doing later. But what I'd really like right now is . . ."

Oh, please say dinner! Please say dinner! Please say dinner!

". . . dinner," she finished.

YES!

So that's what we did. We ordered takeout, and while we waited for it to arrive, The Woman did make one tiny design change to

New Man's penthouse; I mean, *their* penthouse. Or, better yet, *our* penthouse.

On my first-ever visit here, I'd noticed that in the hallway leading to the master bedroom, New Man had family photos on the wall; I'd been particularly struck by the one of who I assumed to be his younger sister. Now The Woman dug out her own framed family photos. New Man found her a hammer and some nails, and beside his family photos, she hung pictures of her parents; her brothers, Tall (the nosy one) and Short (the food-obsessed one), with their own spouses and kids; and me.

Now family photos stretched down the hallway wall as far as my eye could see.

New Man put his arm around The Woman's shoulders. She put her arm around his waist. They tilted their heads together as they looked at the wall.

"Ours," they said at the same time, exhaling happy sighs.

My heart was full to bursting.

Here's the thing about happy families: they can't exist without happy people, and my family was full of them. We had happy people who ate takeout together, and happy people who talked books together, and happy people who shared joint custody of the ol' Gatzer together. What else could one want?

So suck it, Tolstoy. Happy people are infinite in their variety, and fascinating, and fairly devoid of conflict. I don't know about you, but I am living a pretty high life over here. Was there anyone who did happy families better than we did?

I must confess, I was feeling pret-TY smug about that fact.

And as great as I felt then, I felt even better when the doorman called up to say our takeout had arrived.

And that was topped when New Man placed a carton of moo shu chicken on a china plate but left the food in the carton, just the way I like it, and all for me.

I figured maybe New Man would want them to eat their first

meal as cohabitants at the dining room table. Maybe even alone, so they could make out to their hearts' content without me barking my fool head off every time I thought it was going on for too long. But he had other plans.

"I was thinking," he suggested, "movie marathon?"

What could be better? I thought, as he brought the food into the TV room, where the biggest home entertainment system I'd ever seen lived, with a curved screen and everything.

I'll tell you what could be better—he let *me* pick out the movies!

It was a dog-movie marathon from start to finish, with all the greatest hits: *Benji*, *Beethoven*, *The Incredible Journey*, although there is also a cat in that last one. But for once, I didn't mind. In fact, the only time I objected was when New Man tried to offer me a Lassie movie. Color me not a fan. That dog just sets the bar too high. Plus, I'm a city dog. When am I ever going to get a chance to save Timmy from the well? It's just an impossible standard to measure up to.

But the standard of happy people?

We were better than all the people.

We *won* at being people.

Chapter Two

Sunday afternoon

And when The Man came to pick me up on Sunday afternoon? More winning at being happy people!

After The Man and The Woman initially split up, whenever one came to pick me up or drop me off at the other's place, there would always be a whiff of something bittersweet in the air. And later, the first time The Man met New Man, he'd done that overly-firm-handshake thing that guys sometimes do to assert dominance. Which was a mistake since New Man is bigger and built, while if The Man has ever seen the inside of a gym in the years we've been together, no one told me about it. So of course, without even trying to assert dominance, New Man succeeded at it. Plus, he was with The Woman by then. He had nothing to prove.

But now The Man had someone new he was seeing, someone he really liked and who suited him—New Woman!—and The Man seemed more at ease with himself than I'd ever known him to be. No need to dominate anymore; let it all ride.

Which was a good thing since this was his first time picking me up at New Man's since The Woman and I had moved in here, and it was easy to see how someone who lived in a one-bedroom apartment deep in Brooklyn could feel intimidated by someone else, particularly another writer, who had this palatial penthouse.

"Wow," The Man said to New Man, taking in the skyline view. "Well, good for you."

He even seemed to mean it.

Me, I was just pleased that everyone was finally getting along with everyone else.

"I hear tell there's occasion for a 'good for you' too," The Woman told him.

"How's that?"

"I can tell a certain someone is pretty happy with how things are going," she said with a pleased smile.

I figured she was talking about New Woman.

"How can you tell?" The Man said, with a small smile of his own.

And I knew what he meant by that. New Woman, on the occasions I'd met her, wasn't exactly a constant ray of sunshine like The Woman and New Man. Rather, she was the temperamental equal of The Man: cloudy, with an ever-present chance of rain, and just the smidgen of hope that the sun might surprise you.

"All I know is," The Woman said, "that the other day when I told her I had a few revision notes for her, she didn't ask if she should hide all her knives and close all the windows before looking at them. That was a first."

"Good," The Man said, relieved with a touch of happy.

As we took our leave, I marveled again at how well we were all doing at being happy people. And as we slowly strolled home through the lovely afternoon, I reviewed some of the events I'd been present for in The Man's relationship with New Woman thus far and what had brought them to this reasonably happy-for-them moment in time.

After the author event at the 92nd Street Y back in August, The Man had marshaled his courage and asked New Woman if she'd like to have dinner with him one night the following week. I gotta admit, it wasn't such a great ask. It was more like a down-on-yourself, expecting-the-door-to-be-slammed-in-your-face kind of ask. If I had been her, I'd probably have told him no. I mean, I'd never tell him no! I love the guy. I have the advantage, though, of already knowing him, probably better than anybody, including himself, and I know how wonderful he is. But to a new person who doesn't know all that? Yup, I'd have said no.

But she surprised us both and said yes!

"Great," he said, unable to conceal his shock, which was not exactly cool, and yet she oddly seemed to get it. "How about Tuesday? If you tell me where you live, I'll pick you up at seven?"

"No," she said firmly. "How about *you* tell me where *you* live and I'll pick *you* up at seven?"

The way she said it was a touch abrasive, and kind of strange frankly, but then I figured maybe she was thinking: If it turned out The Man was some kind of wacko, she probably wouldn't want him to know where she lived, right? Hey, you can't be too careful. Like The Man himself always says: "Safety first."

When she arrived at seven on Tuesday night, The Man was already waiting, my leash in his hand.

"I was thinking we'd go to Nick's," The Man said, naming the one restaurant we go to regularly because they're dog-friendly.

"I don't know what Nick's is," she said, also looking like she didn't care what Nick's was because she was too busy staring at me. "You didn't tell me you had a dog."

"Nick's is this Italian place and—"

"Good, I love Italian, but you never told me you had a dog."

"I figured you'd assumed. I mean, Gatz was at the event where we met . . ."

"Gatz?"

He nodded.

"Like *The Great Gatsby*?"

More nodding.

"That's cute," she said. "But, no, if I assumed anything, it was that he belonged to my editor and her fiancé. I remember him being with them when I was talking to her after. He tried to . . . *lick* me."

"And you know she's my ex, right?"

Her turn to nod.

"Well," The Man said, "we share joint custody of Gatz. I have him on weekdays and certain holidays."

"Oh. No, I didn't know any of that." Pause. "To tell you the truth, I'm more of a cat person."

It was all I could do not to reel back in horror.

I could see The Man was struggling with this information too.

Neither of us had seen this coming.

Still, when I'd first met New Man, I sensed his fear of me without knowing where it came from—a childhood encounter with an English mastiff that left a small scar on his face. All I knew was: he was leery of me and I sure didn't like him because I wanted The Woman and The Man to get back together, plus, he was *not* The Man. But then a lot of other things happened and we eventually made peace with each other.

But this? A cat person?

"Do you . . . dislike dogs?" The Man asked.

"It's not that," she said. "But I've always been intimidated by the big ones. They seem so unpredictable and, well, big."

"But Gatz isn't like that," The Man said.

Having once stood in the way of The Woman and New Man being together, causing her unhappiness, I never wanted to do that to anyone I loved ever again. So I bit the bullet. I put on my least intimidating face, stuck my tongue out, batted my tail, and gazed at her like I really, really wanted to be her friend.

"No," she said cautiously. "I can see he's not terribly large."

"Maybe if you tried petting him," The Man suggested. "Gatz has never bit anyone, would never bite anyone. But maybe if you'd just pet him, you'd see for yourself just how nonthreatening he is."

I bowed forward, submissively, offering my head up for a scratch.

New Woman crouched down beside me and put a tentative hand to my head. I kept myself from reacting strongly, not even giving off any loudly approving barks because I didn't want to scare her off.

"Not too bad, right?" The Man said encouragingly.

"Not too bad at all," New Woman admitted, sounding surprised and relieved. "You know, he's really not much bigger than a cat."

It took everything I had in me not to react to that one.

"Good thing he's not a rottweiler," New Woman said. "Now, *that* would've been a deal breaker."

Finally, something she and I could agree on. More than once, I'd been grateful to the Universe for not making me a rottweiler.

"So, we can go get dinner?" The Man asked hopefully.

"We can," she agreed, only seeming mildly surprised when she realized The Man fully intended to bring me to dinner with them.

But it was The Man's turn to be surprised when as the dinner neared its completion, and he'd just gotten up the nerve to ask if he could see her again, New Woman said, "You know, whatever this was that we just ate, it doesn't exactly resemble authentic Italian cuisine."

It doesn't? I looked down at the cleared plate where my chicken Parm had been.

"I mean, it's OK," New Woman went on before The Man could respond. "But it's not really authentic. Did you know there are other Italian restaurants in the city?"

Better than this? I looked at my empty plate again.

"But those places won't let me bring Gatz in," The Man finally responded.

"Yes," New Woman said, before reiterating, "but did you know there are places in the city where you can get authentic Italian food, authentic food that tastes amazing?"

I couldn't let The Man remain a bonehead all his life, and I'd already watched him blow one relationship. I wasn't about to sit around while he blew something that looked like it could have potential, not after just one date. Even though I did still have reservations about anyone who referred to themselves as "a cat person."

So before The Man could do the obviously boneheaded thing of reiterating his line, that Nick's was the place to go because Nick's was Gatz-friendly, I nudged his shin hard with my snout to get his attention. When he looked down at me, I hoped my eager eyes were conveying, *Say yes to trying other Italian places*, and because I'm nothing if not self-interested about certain things, I also threw a helping of *And if it is really amazing food, don't forget to bring leftovers home to your good old pal and best wingdog, Gatz*, into my eye-messaging as well. I hoped he got it all.

But he definitely got the first part, because he abruptly said to New Woman, "Yes! I think that . . . Yes! If you'll go out with me again, why not try an, um, entirely different Italian restaurant?"

In response, perhaps recognizing what a huge-for-him concession he'd just made, New Woman half rose from her seat, leaned across the table, and initiated their first kiss, which went on for a long time, their matching backward Mets caps making occasional contact. This was a surprising development because The Man has never been much of one for the ol' PDA; he hates to draw any undue attention to himself. But he sure seemed to be getting into that across-the-table kiss.

Well, what do you know? Someone had compromised, and look at the outstanding results!

So they went on a second date, which The Man told me went even better than the first. I envisioned a string of great dinner dates stretching all the way into eternity. Imagine my shock, then, when for Date #3, The Man told me it was to be a shopping expedition.

But you hate shopping. I frowned at him. I mean, if she got him to change a little bit, it might not be such a bad thing, even though he was already and would always be perfect in my eyes, but I didn't want her changing everything.

"I know, right?" The Man said, laughing. "I do hate shopping. And that's what I told her."

Oh, bad move, dude. A chick asks you out and you tell her you hate the thing she asked you to do?

"I know." The Man laughed again. "I'm a total bonehead sometimes, right?"

Hey, you're the one who said it. I'm just thinking it.

"But get this!" And wouldn't you know it? He laughed some more, and I was beginning to get a little concerned. "I tell her I hate shopping, and she replies, 'So do I!' "

I wasn't sure if I was quite getting this, but I was willing to go with it for a while.

"And that's when she tells me she doesn't want to take me on just any kind of shopping expedition. Oh no. We're going *flannel* shopping." To illustrate, he grabbed at the elbow of the flannel shirt he was wearing open over a T-shirt and jeans, his daily uniform along with his Mets cap; her daily uniform too, as I'd seen. "She tells me she knows all the best places for flannel in town!"

I can't say I shared his excitement to quite the level he did, because I knew that just like finer dining establishments wouldn't want me there, clothing establishments wouldn't be keen to see me either, but I was happy he was happy.

And after their shopping trip, when they returned home with their bags, they even did a little flannel fashion show for me. They bought a lot of flannel, and I can't honestly say I was able to tell one shirt they tried on from another, but it was nice to be included in an activity.

And you know what was even nicer than that?

One day, as The Man and I returned home from him picking

me up at The Woman and New Man's place, we were surprised to find New Woman waiting outside our place.

With Mets tickets in her hands.

The Man looked instantly excited, but then, just as instantly, deflated.

"But I just got Gatz back," he said.

"But it's Mets tickets."

"But I just got Gatz back," he said again.

"But it's Mets tickets."

"But I just got—"

Even I could see that they could go on like this all afternoon and night if they were both determined to remain in their conversational rut, and apparently, she could too, because that's when she shoved the tickets right up under his nose.

"Just look at the tickets," she said.

"But—"

"Look!"

Finally, he did.

And after looking down at them, he brought his eyes back up to look at her.

"It's Bark at the Park?" he said.

"Yes."

"You got us tickets to Bark at the Park at Citi Field?"

"Yes!"

Frankly, this was the most excited I'd ever seen either of them at the same time.

"And if we leave right now," she added, "I think we can get there in time for the part where owners get to parade their dogs around the infield!"

So that's what we did.

And I can't tell you how puffed up my chest got as The Man proudly paraded me around the infield, which I'd never gotten to see up close before, with about four hundred other dogs as New Woman took pictures of us from the sideline. All of us dogs were treated like VIPs—Very Important Puppies—and some of the players even reached out to pet us as we made our rounds. There was a lot of space between me and the dog ahead of me to prevent chasing and doggy mayhem, and it took all my willpower to not trot forward and sniff butt.

Afterward, we sat in the picnic area with all the other dogs and their owners and watched one heckuva game. I got to eat a few hot dogs. Little kids made a fuss over me, even though the ones in our area all had their own dogs with them. I even got to see my favorite pitcher pitch, Jacob deGrom. Two Cy Young Awards to his credit already, and you can just tell Jake's a really good person. The Mets were even winning for him!

I sure was glad there weren't any rottweilers around. Or a cat. It's impossible to picture a ballpark having a Cat Day—that dog won't hunt!

Late in the game, New Woman said she was going for some ice cream. "Would you like some?" she offered The Man.

He nodded.

"How about you, Gatz?"

I stuck my tongue out and panted with glee.

"Make sure his is vanilla," The Man said, unable to tear his eyes from the game. "Dogs can't eat chocolate."

And yet, once she was out of view, The Man did manage to tear his eyes from the game, turning his attention to me.

"She's pretty great, isn't she?" he asked, a wide smile growing across his face.

I thumped my tail enthusiastically. How could I disagree? She'd brought me to the ballpark; she was buying me ice cream. What was not to like? And she was doing all this even though I knew that when she'd first met me, she'd been a bit hesitant because, well, I'm a dog. I thumped my tail more energetically.

"Yeah, that's what I think too," The Man said. "Which is why I'm considering—just considering, mind you!—asking her to move in with us. What do you think?"

Honestly, I didn't know what to think then. Sure, they'd had a bunch of good dates. Sure, they'd each made some compromises. But wasn't this all a bit sudden? I mean, he'd rushed into things with The Woman, and look how that turned out.

Plus, didn't New Woman tell us she was a cat person?

What could *that* mean???

Chapter Three

October

It was time for that monthly event known as Book Club, formerly held at The Woman's old place and this month being held for the first time at the place we now shared with New Man.

As The Woman's trio of coworkers entered—The Blonde, The Redhead, The Brunette—they took turns oohing and aahing over the view.

I waited beside them during the oohing and aahing, thumping my tail impatiently. It's not that I was over the view—who could ever be over that?—but I was impatient to get to the heart of the evening. I'm not talking about the book, which I hadn't read yet. I'm talking about the food.

Previously, on the consumption front, Book Club evenings had involved copious amounts of red wine (not for me) and copious amounts of nachos (definitely for me). New Man, however, had decided to kick the food part up a notch. And while I have historically been resistant to the forces of inevitable change, I found myself eager to try the finger foods he'd prepared: blackened shrimp avocado bites, which were supposed to be paired with cucumber, but he knows I'm not a fan so he left that part out; caprese empanadas with tomato, mozzarella, and basil; and little veggie egg cups, with the cheese and veggies surrounded by the cutest little phyllo crusts, kind of like mini quiches.

The first time New Man had attended Book Club, he'd tried to help out in The Woman's kitchen. He'd seemed to experience confusion over how to properly put together nachos and even more confusion about the relationship between spoons and fruit. At the time, I'd judged him for it, thinking him a try-hard who was trying too hard to impress her. But I've since come to realize that there's nothing wrong with going the extra mile, doing everything you can to impress someone you care about. Frankly, The Man could use a bit more of that quality, since one of the ways The Man blew it with The Woman was by not being gung ho enough—or at all, really—about spending holidays with family.

But since getting to know New Man, I'd come to realize that he was very comfortable in the kitchen; a gourmet, even. Was there anything the guy couldn't do? Honestly, it'd be so easy to hate someone who's so perfect in everyone else's eyes, but the truth of the matter is, for all of New Man's legion talents and accomplishments and swoony good looks, the guy doesn't have an ego about anything. So yeah, I love the guy now too.

OK, back to Book Club and those assembled. All three worked with The Woman at the publishing house where she was a rock star editor. The Brunette works in Accounting, is odd, has a penchant for buying snakes, and loves dancing the Charlie Brown with beautiful men. Art department is the domain of The Redhead, who has a practical side and was the one to figure out what should be done when The Woman and New Man started to like-like each other while she was still his editor. And then there is The Blonde, the stiff enforcer of Book Club etiquette who is now New Man's editor even though she's not as good an editor as The Woman.

Everyone was still on their first glass of wine and talking about the story arc, which I had no opinion on, having not read the book, and I was on my third blackened shrimp avocado bite.

"When the manicurist turned out to be the killer?" The Blonde remarked. "I was really impressed by the setup."

"I dunno." The Brunette took a sip of her wine. "It made me think about my manicurist, and how she's always had this beady-eye thing going on? I'm nervous to go back."

The Woman's phone started to ring. Usually, for Book Club, she kept her phone turned off, since she wasn't raised by wolves. But when she looked at her phone, a puzzled expression bordering on dismay furrowed her pretty brow.

The Blonde, oblivious to The Woman's look of puzzlement, looked across the room at The Brunette and focused her attention on her next sip of wine. "I'm surprised you'd think that far into it."

"What is that supposed to mean?"

"You don't exactly pay attention to detail."

"Excuse me?"

The Woman, oblivious to the exchange between her friends, which wasn't anything new, was squinting at her screen. "What is this?"

"What?" New Man asked.

"Guys, come on—" The Redhead interjected.

"You brought chips tonight," The Blonde spat at The Brunette.

"So?"

"I said I'd bring chips. You're trying to sabotage me."

"Some person on Twitter with the username @SimplySimantha tagged me with a post calling me a predator," The Woman said loud enough to cut through the noise. Everyone looked up at her and forgot their petty differences.

"What?" asked The Redhead.

"Who could ever think you were a predator?" The Brunette questioned.

"I don't know." The Woman looked over her phone, lost. "I . . . I guess it's about being in a relationship with one of my previous authors."

Just then, The Blonde and New Man exchanged a meaningful look.

"Do you think it could be related to . . ." The Blonde said.

"I don't see how it could be," New Man responded.

"What?" The Woman said. "What are you two talking about?"

"The other day," The Blonde started, "at that book event . . ."

Apparently, there'd been an author/editor book event that The Blonde and New Man had participated in. Normally, The Woman would have gone along with New Man for moral support, but she'd been feeling a bit under the weather, and so she'd stayed away until she was sure whatever she had wasn't catching. She's very considerate that way.

"When we got to the Q and A part," New Man continued, "this bizarre woman immediately leaped to her feet and started asking questions about you."

"*Me*?" The Woman said.

"She said she'd heard I was engaged to my editor," New Man said, "and she went on to explain that it was the most unethical thing she'd ever heard of."

"That's when I explained that you weren't his editor anymore, that I was," The Blonde said.

"But still, she wouldn't let it go," New Man said. "She wanted to know at exactly what point you'd stopped being my editor."

"I reassured her that as soon as you two realized there was a romantic spark between you, you passed him off to me," The Blonde said. "Not that I minded."

Indeed. I knew that part had been hard on The Woman, who loves her work and who had been excited at the prospect of helping New Man take his writing to the next level, which was something he'd badly wanted to do. But they'd both given that part of the dream up in exchange for True Love, with the accompanying hope that The Blonde would rise to the occasion and be equal to the task.

"We both thought we handled it very well," New Man said, "but she simply wouldn't let it go."

"But when she started in on sexual harassment, unequal power, and #MeToo," The Blonde said, "thankfully, the crowd finally shot her down. Another woman said her claims were invalid since he switched editors, and another guy added that he came in the hopes of getting tips on how to get published, and we all managed to move on from the awkward moment."

The Woman looked gobsmacked and I could relate.

"And you didn't see fit, either of you," she said, shifting her gaze from one to the other, "to tell me about this?"

They both winced, then shrugged.

"It wasn't like that," The Blonde said.

"You hadn't been feeling well," New Man said.

"We'd handled it," The Blonde said.

"Why upset you," New Man said, "when it was over?"

"But what if it's not?" The Woman said, waving the screen at the assembled again. "Do you think this could have something to do with that?"

"Let me see that," The Redhead said, taking the phone. "Look," she remarked, "even if it is somehow the same person, @SimplySimantha is a nobody. There's not even a profile picture. If Twitter still used the default eggs, she'd be just another egg."

"And see?" The Brunette said. "This person doesn't have any followers, zero," she added, evincing the math skills that had landed her in the Accounting department. "No one's ever going to see this nonsense if she has no followers. No one's listening to her."

"You should block her," The Redhead said.

The Woman moved to do just that but then stopped. "If I do that, I won't see if she says anything else. Isn't it better to be forewarned so I can be forearmed?"

"I don't see why you'd want to torture yourself like that," The Redhead said. "It's just some troll."

"Still," The Woman said.

"I'm sure it'll all blow over," New Man said encouragingly. "It's nothing."

"You're right," The Woman said, starting to brighten. It's tough to keep her down.

"We did nothing wrong," New Man said, adding with even greater emphasis, "*You* did nothing wrong."

After a round of encouraging "of course not" comments, I thought we'd return to discussing the book, but they had other things in mind.

"Any more planning progress on the wedding?" The Redhead asked eagerly, leaning forward with elbows on the table while cradling her chin in her hands.

"We were thinking maybe New Year's Eve?" The Woman said, looking at New Man.

"I went to a New Year's wedding once. The cake—completely froze over. It was inedible. They had to order . . . *pudding*," The Brunette contributed with a shudder.

"Well," New Man said diplomatically, "nothing's carved in stone yet."

As they continued to discuss this happy topic, I felt annoyed at @SimplySimantha for having briefly disturbed Book Club, a monthly evening usually characterized by bonhomie. But then I thought: *Why be annoyed? Why be worried?* I wasn't worried. None of us were.

We were happy, and no one, not even some egg on Twitter, could get in the way of that.

Chapter Four

Still October

For the first time, it was brought to my attention that New Woman wasn't just "a cat person," odious as that phrase might be, but that she did, in fact, actually *have* a cat.

"Look, Gatz," The Man said to me, brushing my fur in a clear attempt to make me appear perfectly groomed. For himself, he had on one of the new flannels he'd bought with New Woman, which, I had to admit, was even softer than the flannels he used to buy on his own.

"If I'm going to ask her to move in with us," he went on, *brush, brush,* "it's not enough for just me to wanna do it. You have to be on board with it too. You know, I would never willingly subject you to a living situation you weren't okay with."

I liked New Woman well enough. I sincerely wanted The Man to be happy. So where was the beef?

"The thing is," *brush, brush,* "she's got this cat."

???

"So if we ask her to move in with us—which I haven't done yet!—I don't see how we can avoid the cat moving in with us too. That's why I invited us over to her place tonight for dinner, so you could meet the cat, see what you think first."

Have you met this cat? I thought. *What's this cat like?*

Then I realized that of course he had. I knew he'd been to her place before without me. Even if he hadn't told me about it, I'd have been able to guess because he always came back from her place with a moony look in his eyes and added pep in his stride. Plus, he smelled different. So of course he'd met the cat. I raised my eyebrows at him questioningly.

"He's a mackerel tabby," The Man said. "He's OK." He sighed. "His name is Hoops."

Hoops? What the heck kind of name was that for a cat? It wasn't even literary!

"Yeah, I know," The Man said, sighing again. "I didn't name him."

Clearly.

"I know it's a lot to ask," The Man said, cradling my face in his hands and scratching me under my chin, just the way I like it. "But I think I really like her. I mean, I know I like her, maybe even love her. So, could you try? Could you try for me?"

Of course I would try for him. Who did he think he was dealing with here? Didn't he know by now that I'd do anything for him?

Even make nice with a cat named Hoops.

So I thumped my tail vociferously, panted even more vociferously to show my willingness and eagerness to play nice with Hoops, and we were off.

I had no idea how far we were going to be walking, but it turned out to be not very far at all. Apparently, except for New Man, all writers live in Brooklyn.

Despite my thoroughly understandable trepidation about Hoops, I found myself feeling excited as The Man knocked. One of the things I love about the city is the incredible range of smells and stimulation encountered when outdoors. And, despite my hesitancy about change, I love encountering new indoor spaces too. You never know what great new smells there might be, what objects you might turn into toys, what tasty morsels you might find forgotten under a couch or in a corner due to indifferent housekeeping. I'm secretly a fan of indifferent housekeeping, just so long as it doesn't lapse into sloth or run the risk of the health department showing up. But rarely did I get taken to new-to-me indoor spaces.

New Woman's place did not disappoint. It was smaller than ours, but more nicely decorated, with those homey touches that mean so much: recently fluffed cushions, hors d'oeuvres already laid out, and a nod to color coordination, an area of expertise The Man is sorely lacking in.

I didn't make it far into the apartment when I came into contact with *him*. Hoops the Cat was standing tall, guarding New Woman in the kitchen. I tried letting my tongue loll out in a friendly manner, but Hoops was having none of it. We were in a stare-down. He hissed at me, not a reaction I'm used to, but rather than barking in his face as would have been only natural when faced with such hostile behavior, I kind of understood where the little dude was coming from. This was his space and he had to let me know it. So instead I simply kept my distance and didn't let it annoy me when, as I began to explore the place, he trailed my every move. Again, who could blame the little guy?

Plus, unlike the wild cats I occasionally encountered on the streets of the city, this one had clearly been domesticated, making him no real threat, all hiss and no bite. More than that, I'd once heard Mick Jagger say—when asked how he could still run around and dance all over the stage at his age—that anyone can do anything for an hour. While I think Mick might have been overestimating what other not-Mick beings are capable of in advancing years, I could relate to the general sentiment. I could tolerate Hoops for an hour—a few hours, even!—but the jury was still out on how I'd feel about having the little guy underfoot full-time. And when he got more comfortable with me and started sniffing my butt, he was stretching my limits. *I* sniff butt. I don't *get* sniffed.

But back to hors d'oeuvres. Did I mention there were hors d'oeuvres? That's the major way New Woman's place didn't disappoint—the smells! Once I'd managed to finally create some physical distance between myself and Hoops, I made straight for that coffee table.

There were cheese and crackers, mini beef empanadas—is it just me, or was I being offered empanadas everywhere I went all of a sudden?—and Swedish meatballs. I put my paws up on the table, trying to decide what to go for first.

"Gatz!" The Man yelled, using a rare admonitory tone. "You know better than to jump up and steal hors d'oeuvres!"

Or dervs? It's not pronounced *whores de-vores*??? I'd been doing that for years!

"That's OK," New Woman said. "Hoops does that kind of thing too. But first he always pulls a napkin down from the table, like setting a little place for himself on the floor for me to serve him on. I was telling a friend about it one time at the dining table and I could tell she didn't believe me until, right while I was still telling her about it, a furry paw appeared over the corner of the table, yanking down one of the napkins." She paused. "Um, how would Gatz prefer to be served?"

"Um, a plate would be good," The Man said. "He's not much of a napkin guy."

Actually, I was more of an I-don't-mind-eating-right-off-the-floor guy, and The Man had never minded that about me, but I could see what he was going for here. He was hoping we'd come off as *civilized*.

"Here," The Man said, taking the small plate she offered him. "I can take care of that. He'd probably like a little bit of everything."

He knew me so well. I do have eclectic tastes when it comes to dining. But I knew that cats were supposed to be finicky eaters, they're always saying as much in all those commercials, so I thought I'd have a little fun with Hoops, using my snout to push a hunk of horseradish cheese off my plate and onto his napkin. Sure, I'd eat it. I'd eat almost anything. Heck, I'd been known to eat shoes back in my puppy days! I figured the cat would be put off by the smell alone, maybe even enough to disappear for a bit. Well, color me surprised.

The cat liking horseradish cheese was a plot development that neither I nor the cat saw coming.

Here's another plot development I hadn't seen coming: that The Man should prove so abysmally bad at reading a room. I mean, yes, he's always been socially challenged, but he's not a complete moron.

But as hors d'oeuvres turned to dinner—and, yes, fine, it was cute when Hoops did his little napkin trick at the dining room table—and then to dessert time, The Man seemed to grow more and more eager.

New Woman had just gone to the kitchen to get the cheesecake when he turned to me.

"You and Hoops doing OK?" he whispered.

Yes, but—

"This could work out, right?"

Yes, eventually, but—

"Yeah, that's what I think too."

Dude, you're not even reading me right anymore!

"I think so too!"

Aargh!!!

"So, Gatz and I were thinking," The Man began, as New Woman came back with her cheesecake.

You. You were thinking. Not me.

"How would you and Hoops like to move in with me and Gatz?"

Too soon! Too soon! And since when do you put "me" before "Gatz"? That's lousy grammar!

Apparently, I wasn't the only one appalled by his shocking use of grammar, because New Woman almost dropped her cheesecake.

"This is too soon," she said, after taking a brief moment to recover.

It's too soon!

"But I thought . . ." The Man started to say, instantly crestfallen.

After wisely setting down the cheesecake first, she covered his hands with both of hers.

"Look," she said, "I like you." Before he could object to that paltry "like," she added, "Even more than that; you know I do. But I think it's a little too early. We've only been dating for what—two months?"

He looked skyward, doing the math, nodding when he realized her math was good. Maybe she'd be able to help him understand his royalty statements.

"Plus," she said, "I've never lived with anyone before."

"Never?"

"Well, duh. I mean, of course, first I lived with my family while growing up. Then, in college, I had roommates. And after college but before I could afford my own place, I had even more roommates. But I've never lived with a man or a woman I was dating before."

"Like, as in never?"

"That's what I said. And I'm not starting now."

"What about after, say, many more months? You know, if things keep going well."

"Nope."

The poor guy. He just didn't know what to do with this brick wall.

"Look," she explained, "you may not have realized this about me before, but I'm a little conservative."

"You mean . . . ?" He raised his eyebrows.

"Gosh, no. No, no, no, no, no. That's spelled with a small c. But I also grew up Catholic and that's spelled with the big C."

"And that means . . . in this context . . ."

"I will never live with anyone, romantically, without being married first."

"But you'll have sex without being married first?"

Now it was time for us all to do the duh / eye roll thing, even Hoops. I'd heard them shake the mattress at our place and no doubt Hoops had heard them shake the mattress at her place, although when she was at our place, she never stayed the whole night.

"Duh," she said. "I'm Catholic and in my thirties. I'm not a nun."

"I gotta admit to being a bit lost at this point," The Man said. "So what are you suggesting—that we get married?"

Well, who could really blame her for laughing in his face right then?

"God, no!" she said, still laughing. "It's too soon for anything like that."

Too soon, see? That's what I'd tried to tell the guy. This was all too soon.

"What, then?" he said, curiously uninsulted by her laughter.

"For us to live together, we'd need to be married first. But for us to even consider that step, things would need to be a lot more serious than they are now."

"How so?"

"You'd need to do things, like, I don't know, introduce me to your family. And of course you'd need to meet mine too, which is a whole other kettle of fish."

"That doesn't sound too bad . . ." The Man started to say hesitantly, which showed just how heavily into her he was. The Man hates spending time with his family, something I don't blame him for—they are a *cold* kettle of fish.

Where were all these fish references coming from all of a sudden? Clearly, I was spending too much time with the cat.

"Oh, and courting," she added quickly. "You'd need to properly court me."

"*Court* you?"

Was he being deliberately thick now? Even I knew what courting was. It's all that Romeo and Juliet hearts-and-flowers shit—or sometimes Romeo and Romeo or Juliet and Juliet—but hopefully with no one taking poison in the end.

"Yes, courting!" she said, with the same exasperation I was feeling with his thickness. "You need to take me on real, non-Nick's dates."

"We went to a different Italian place."

"One time!" She raised a finger in the air to make her point.

"What else?"

"It's not for me to tell you. You need to figure it out for yourself. All I know is, all the romantic relationships I've had thus far have failed. Obviously. And they've all failed from a lack of effort."

The Man gulped.

"So you're asking me to change," he said.

"*No.* I would never do that. But I am expecting you to try and I am asking you to figure things out. For yourself."

"And while I'm doing that?"

"Oh, I'll be figuring things out for myself too."

The Man gulped again, but then covered one of her hands with one of his, indicating to all concerned that he was willing to consider all this, that he was willing to at least try.

Me, I did no gulping, because this had all come with a reprieve for Hoops and me. Neither of us would have to deal with permanently living together right now and could thus go the Mick Jagger route: work your tail off for an hour (or a bit longer), knowing you'll be able to get off the stage when the night is through.

Ah, who knew what the cat made of the whole situation?

Chapter Five

Still October!

Even though none of us are Scandinavian, we were getting our *hygge* on.

In practical terms, for us, it meant that when The Woman and New Man came through the door, they immediately took off their outside-world clothes. Well, maybe not immediately. It's not like they did it right off the penthouse elevator. But they did take off their shoes, put on what they called their "comfies," and put on fuzzy socks since there was a distinct nip in the air.

After a hearty meal of beef stew made by New Man, who did inform us that once he was back in writing mode there would be takeout for the foreseeable future, we'd all settled into the couch, the two of them close together, feet up, fleece throw blankets across their laps.

Me, I was also curled up in fleece, a new throw blanket that New Man had recently brought home for me—cream-colored with little border collie heads and the word "arf" all over the place, and fringe that was great for chasing—so I could be *hygge* too.

There came a moment of group contented silence, broken when The Woman said:

"Here's something we've never discussed."

"Mmm . . ."

"Kids."

My ears perked up, and there went my feelings of *hygge*.

"I'm sure we have," New Man said.

"I'm equally sure we haven't."

I adjusted my seating on the couch to face them, my heart racing in my chest. Why was this conversation making me so anxious?

"But how is that possible? I thought we've talked about everything important. Where we stand on politics . . ."

"In total agreement, thankfully."

"What order the newspaper should be tackled in . . ."

"Crossword puzzle, editorials, front page, arts, business, sports."

"Unless a team we like played the night before, in which case it goes box scores first but then everything else remains the same."

"I would never dispute that."

"Which is the best Gabriel García Márquez book . . ."

"And you're still wrong."

"I'm not. It's *One Hundred Years of Solitude*."

"Wrong, wrong, wrong. It's *Love in the Time of Cholera*. You know I'm right."

Okay, get to the point, get to the point . . .

"Well, maybe," he conceded. "You're sure we never talked about kids?"

"I promise you; I would remember."

So would I!

"So, where do we stand on it?"

"You first."

"Well . . ." he started, carefully considering. "I always pictured myself being a dad one day. But of course, if you don't feel the same . . ."

"Then what? You'd leave me?" she asked with a laugh.

"Don't be absurd," he said, but not unkindly. "If you didn't, it might take me a moment to reprogram my vision for the future, but

I'd get there. The most important thing in the world to me is you. Anything else good that comes my way is extra. But you will always be enough. You are enough."

"I know that. I just wanted to hear it said out loud."

"And I was happy to oblige."

"Anyway, you won't need to reprogram your vision for the future because I feel the same. About having kids, I mean. But everything else too, of course."

I was shocked.

I mean, I knew that human beings had a tendency to reproduce . . . but, somehow, I never thought it might happen in any household I was a part of! I loved kids when I saw them on the street, and I really loved The Woman's nieces and nephews. And I really, really loved the way all those kids loved me back. So that part could be cool. But did I really want the competition?

"I'm glad you brought it up," New Man said.

"I'm glad we're in agreement," The Woman said. "But here's something else I need to know if we're in agreement on."

"Hmm . . ." he said, nuzzling her neck.

"Is it too cold out to be eating ice cream?"

He stopped nuzzling. "It is never, ever too cold out to be eating ice cream."

"Good, I'll go get us some," she said, rising.

"And I'll go get us some more fleece, just in case we need it," he said, rising too.

My stomach was doing backflips, and I'm not one for gymnastics. How could they possibly want a kid?

I didn't have much time to mull it over—I guess it's quicker to grab a few throws than to scoop ice cream—because he returned quicker than she did. Good thing one of them did, because her phone had started pinging, pinging so fast and so furious that it was practically skating across the coffee table.

"What's this?" he said, picking it up, as she returned with three bowls of vanilla ice cream, only two of them with hot fudge on top.

"What?" she said.

"You'd better look," he said, handing her phone over.

"Oh no," she said in dismay. "Now that @SimplySimantha account is tagging book bloggers with her 'predator' tweet, and some of them are actually reposting it. People are believing this!"

"What do you want to do?"

"I don't know. Should I report her?"

"That's a good idea. Maybe they'll take her page down."

"Is it that easy, though, to get someone's page taken down?"

"Honestly? I don't know."

"I mean, wouldn't she actually need to be saying something dangerous or threatening, instead of throwing unsubstantiated rumors recklessly about?"

"Probably . . . but who in their right mind would listen to unsubstantiated rumors?"

The Woman nodded uncertainly. She tried to shake it off.

"I'm not going to let it bother me. It'll blow over, right?"

"Of course it will."

They may have been in agreement, but even with ice cream and a fleece throw, somehow, I sensed there would be no more *hygge* for me that night.

Chapter Six

Still October . . .

The Man was in a dither.

Not only was he still all worked up about what New Woman had told him when we went to dinner at her place, basically saying he'd need to step up his game if there was to be any hope for them having a future together, but now his editor had called and said he wanted to stop by with some notes for him.

It's my understanding that most authors would kill to get in-office face time with their editors and the other publishing house people responsible for their books. And, being situated in New York, it would be easy enough for The Man to do. But he's never been about what's easy in terms of anything social. He just doesn't have the schmooze gene. His editor knows this about him and so, reluctantly, comes to us.

Soon the doorbell rang and there was The Editor.

It used to be that The Editor and I didn't like each other very much. For my part, I found him to be too tweedy, which I translated into pretentious. Plus, he always seemed to leave The Man more miserable than he'd found him. I don't know what his problem with me was. But then one thing and another happened, and I'd come to the realization that The Editor simply wanted what The Man wanted: for The Man to wind up with the best book he could possibly write. It wasn't really his fault if his role in that equation sometimes caused The Man pain. It was all for art.

So, no, I wasn't about to jump in the guy's lap anytime soon, but I'd come around some.

"Hey," The Man let out uneasily.

"Don't look so excited to see me," The Editor said, manuscript pages in hand.

I arfed a hello to let him know I was there too.

"Oh, hello, Gatz," he said.

After he entered, the door was closed, libations in the form of beer were offered and declined with an I'd-prefer-wine sniff, and it was time to get down to business.

"But I thought you loved this book," The Man said anxiously, adjusting and readjusting his butt on the couch cushions.

"I do love this book," The Editor said. "It's simply that, upon my most recent read, it occurred to me that there are some improvements you could make."

"You've got cavils."

"I've got cavils."

Oh no! Not cavils!

"I promise you," The Editor said, "it's not a lot. But I do think that were you to expend just a little more elbow grease on it, well, who knows where this one could take you."

"I'm actually pretty OK with where I am."

"Oh, come on. No author wants to remain midlist their whole career."

The Man just looked back at him.

The Man and I, we were pretty content to remain midlist. Just so long as the money from books kept this roof over our heads and enough kibble in the ol' kibble bowl, what more did we need?

"Who knows?" The Editor pressed on. "They might find it in the budget to send you out on a real tour with this one."

And now terror slowly seeped out onto The Man's face.

"Fine," The Editor said. "We can talk about that another time. For now, could we just . . ."

He adjusted his horn-rimmed glasses before consulting his notes and getting into his cavils.

I must confess, my mind wandered then. I love a good story as much as the next dog, but you know how it is: I don't need to know how the sausages get made.

So as The Editor droned on about the subplot, I let my mind focus on more pleasant thoughts, like *mmm . . . sausages . . .*

The Man's mind must have been wandering elsewhere too, because both our attentions were drawn back to The Editor when The Editor reached out and gently tapped The Man on the Mets cap with his red pencil.

"Hello?" The Editor tried. "Anyone at home in there?"

"Oh, sorry," The Man said. "I guess I wandered for a bit."

"I could tell."

"Sorry, again. You could?"

"Yes. Usually by this point, you'd have pushed back on my notes at least a dozen times. What's wrong?"

The Man took a big breath in and out. "It's my . . . *relationship*." He proceeded to slowly mumble about wanting New Woman to move in, her saying she'd never live with a romantic partner before marriage, and even worse than that, her desire to be courted.

To his credit, The Editor listened to it all with a great deal of patience. Really, this guy was growing on me more and more.

So it was a shame to hear him say, once The Man was done talking, "It's hard to believe you've reached the age you have without knowing how to properly court someone."

Hey now!

"Hey now!" The Man said.

"Sorry," The Editor said. "Sometimes I guess I could use an editor. Still, aren't there any role models you could use for this?"

"Like who exactly?"

"Your parents? I'm pretty sure you've said they're still together."

The Man snorted.

Who could blame him? From everything I'd heard, they were awful.

"OK, not them, then," The Editor said, accurately reading the room. He removed his glasses, closed his eyes, and pinched the bridge of his nose. "I'm sure I'll hate myself in the morning for this," he said. Then he put his glasses back on. "But why don't you come to my place for dinner sometime?"

The Man paused, looking at The Editor skeptically. "I've never been to your place."

"Yes. I know. And while I had fully intended to keep it that way, my husband and I have been together since college. Twenty-five years in, we're still content, happy even. Most people we know say ours is one of the most successful relationships they've ever seen."

Just then, The Man's phone buzzed. Looking at it, he said, "Oh! It's her! I better take this."

Rising from his seat, he began frantically pacing the room, and we could only hear his side of the conversation, which consisted of stuff like "Hey" and "I'm absolutely working on it already" and "Oh, I've got a whole, um, master plan." But then his voice turned panicky as he said, "What is it?"

After an awkwardly long pause, he cupped his hand around the microphone and turned his back to us. But even though he did all that and lowered his voice, it's not like he left the room, so it's not like we couldn't hear him when he began crooning softly.

It didn't take me long to figure out what he was singing to New Woman.

After all, we'd seen the movie on TCM just the week before.

"Goin' Courtin'"? Dude, you're singing her "Goin' Courtin'" from Seven Brides for Seven Brothers*?*

Having never gone courting myself, I don't claim to be any authority. But even I knew that it had to involve more than, literally through song, declaring that's what you were doing.

And what's New Woman making of the parts about shooting a gun and catching a rabbit? You don't hunt! And that's not romantic!

What ever happened to show, don't tell? He was supposed to show her his love through courting, not just tell it by singing the word "courting"—or, more specifically, "courtin' "—like that would somehow magically do the trick.

The Editor and I exchanged mildly horrified glances, so imagine our shock when, just as soon as The Man finished his ditty, we could hear New Woman laughing loudly through the phone. Then the laughing stopped, and he went quiet as she told him some things.

Perhaps realizing that it wasn't going to get any better than that at the moment, he quickly got off the phone by telling her that he had to go because his editor was here.

"Well," The Editor said, "at least she didn't sound as horrified by that performance as we were. She sounded like she might have been charmed."

"She said it was cute," The Man said with wonder. "She said *I* was cute." But then the wonder left his eyes as panic returned. "But she also said it wasn't what she'd had in mind."

"Did she mention anything about 'show, don't tell'?" The Editor asked.

Glumly, The Man nodded. "How'd you know?"

That's when The Editor reiterated his invitation for The Man to come have dinner with him and his husband at his place.

"I . . . I don't know," The Man said. "So, what, you'd be my . . . *role models*?"

"I don't see anyone else offering. Who knows? Maybe you'll learn something."

"And when would this, uh, educational dinner take place?"

The Editor shrugged. “No point in delaying it too long and giving you time to blow it with this woman. How about this weekend?”

The Man’s hand went to his neck and he started rubbing the skin there, a telltale sign of nerves. “Um, but I don’t have Gatz on the weekends.”

The Editor looked at him. “And there’s your problem right there, or at least one of them: you won’t go practically anywhere unless you can bring that dog.”

Hey!

And yet, he kind of had a point. Much as I love to go with, pretty much anywhere and everywhere, I could see where maybe I was limiting The Man’s options with New Woman. Sometimes.

But as The Man commenced to rub his neck even harder, and we all had to acknowledge that the idea of going to a new-to-him place alone was causing The Man’s anxiety to escalate, The Editor let out a relenting sigh.

“Fine, we’ll do it early next week,” said The Editor, looking down at me. “And he can come too.”

The Man instantly brightened as he consulted me. “Does that sound good to you, Gatz?”

See? The Man was *trying*. The Man was more than willing to try. I lolled out my tongue and let my best doggy smile shine.

Chapter Seven

Still October . . .

When The Woman arrived to pick me up from The Man's that Friday, although he was still absorbed in his own self-absorption, one look at her face and even he could tell that something wasn't right.

"What's wrong?" he asked.

"It's nothing."

When a woman says it's nothing, you know there's gotta be something.

He stepped closer to her in the doorway, looking down into her eyes.

"Come on," he said carefully. "You can still talk to me."

"I know that," she said, sighing. "It's . . . something at work." She forced a bright smile. "But no worries. It'll sort itself out. Somehow."

"Well, if you change your mind . . ."

"I'll let you know."

He lent her a knowing smile. She lent him a knowing smile.

And we were off.

When we arrived at the penthouse shortly thereafter, The Woman yelled out a "Hello?" to New Man but received no answer.

With a disappointed shrug, she said, "Maybe he popped out for groceries."

I figured that she was disappointed that he wasn't there, not only because she wanted to see his handsome face, but also because she really did need to talk to someone.

That gave me an idea.

I trotted off toward the hallway leading to the master bedroom. Halfway there, I stopped and looked back at her, gave out a little bark.

"What is it, Gatz?"

I trotted some more, stopped again, looked back.

That did the trick. She got the message.

This time when I trotted the rest of the way to my destination, I could hear her following me until I stopped in front of a photo of her with her brothers. Then I let out two barks.

Looking up at the photo, she broke out into a big smile. She bent down for another face nuzzle.

"Gatz, you always have the best ideas."

She texted them both that she needed to talk, then got out her laptop, and before you know it, we were all in with a Zoom.

The Woman's family moved here from England when she was small, but for some reason, even though she still has her British accent, they lost theirs and sound as American as apple pie. People are surprised to learn they're all from the same family, but trust me, they are.

And there they were on our screen, Tall looking concerned while Short chomped on a drumstick that Henry VIII wouldn't have turned up his drinker's nose at.

"Oh, I'm sorry," The Woman said. "You should've said you were in the middle of dinner. I could've waited."

"It's not dinner," Short said around a mouthful of poultry.

"It's not?"

"It's dessert."

"What's wrong?" Tall asked.

The Woman launched into the tale thus far, everything that @SimplySimantha had been up to.

And then came the new development.

"This woman and the bloggers have started tagging my publishing house about it too, demanding that something be done. It's starting to make me nervous," she admitted. "What should I do?"

"Maybe it's not as bad as you think," Short said.

"Maybe we should look at Twitter," Tall said, picking up his phone to do so. "It's never good when they go after your employer."

Short put his drumstick down long enough to open Twitter on his phone as well. I thought maybe he should've wiped his greasy fingers on a napkin first, but, hey, it wasn't my place.

"Oh." Tall scrolled. "This is bad."

"You need to get off Twitter," Short said. "That place is a cesspool."

"But you love Twitter!" The Woman said.

"Of course I love Twitter," Short said. "But I only use it to talk about politics, *General Hospital*, and puppies. Something like this, though . . ." Short shook his head ruefully.

"I hate to say it," Tall said, "but he's right. You need to stop looking at this thing."

"Don't you think I should respond, though?" she asked anxiously.

"*NO!*" they shouted in unison, for once in full agreement on something.

"That's the last thing you should ever do," Short said.

"But shouldn't I defend myself?"

"*NO!*" came the unified cry a second time.

"Whatever you say," Short said, "it'll get taken out of context."

"Even if you consult a lawyer first and come up with what you *think* is the perfectly worded response, it'll get taken out of context," Tall said. "People will tear you apart."

"It's best to say nothing at all," Short said.

"Give it time to die down," Tall said.

"Do you really think it will?" The Woman said hopefully.

"It has to," Tall said. "You did nothing wrong."

"Just stay off Twitter," Short said. "If you don't see it, it's not happening. And if you don't respond to it, if you don't give the mob any satisfaction, they'll have to move on to someone else. They always do."

"I guess that sounds like a plan," The Woman said, "of sorts."

Short picked up his drumstick again, chomped.

"Here's what I want to know," Tall said.

"Hmm?" The Woman said.

"What's being alleged," Tall said, "that you're a predator, that your relationship is unethical, even though we all know it didn't go down that way . . ."

"I don't see the question in there," The Woman said.

"It's just . . ." Tall said. "There are *two* of you in this relationship . . . Why are *you* the only one being targeted?"

The Woman sat there for a moment, silent. I supposed the thought hadn't occurred to her.

"You know . . ." she said, "I don't know."

Chapter Eight

Gotta love October!

The guy who answered The Editor's door was not what we expected. Where The Editor was trim, horn-rimmed, and tweedy, with close-cropped hair, this guy was much taller, burlier, the opposite of tweedy, and with a mop top of hair that looked, well, kind of like a mop. And he came equipped with a dish towel draped over one shoulder.

"Oh, hey," he said with a voice like a bassoon and a generous smile, "we were expecting you. I'll let him know you're here." Brief pause and then, "Hey!" he yelled into the space behind him, before stepping aside and granting us entrance.

Ah, I thought, stepping over the threshold, *that must be The Husband*.

My immediate impression was: *Wow, someone here really loves books.* There were bookshelves everywhere, even in the entryway, the shelves so overstuffed, there were more books crammed in and lying across the tops of the books that were spine out. There were more books on every surface with the exception of the dining room table, which I could glimpse through open pocket doors, and there were even stacks of paperbacks on the floor. The floors themselves were dark hardwood throughout, with the occasional fringed rug. There wasn't a single piece of seating that wasn't overstuffed, making them so enticing, and every lamp gave off a warm glow. The whole place seemed designed for comfort and knowledge.

Well, I was impressed.

I was also impressed by the smells of food wafting through the air, until, underlying it all, I caught the whiff of . . .

Was that *cat*?

I started barking, loudly, and, I'm ashamed to admit, somewhat berserkly.

"He must smell Arturo," The Editor said, entering.

"Named after Pérez-Reverte," said The Husband.

"One of our favorite authors," The Editor added.

Honestly, if someone had warned me there was going to be a cat here, I wouldn't have been reacting this way. A dog does need to be warned about this stuff.

"He died recently," The Husband said.

Oh. I ceased my berserk barking. I didn't want to be disrespectful.

"I'm so sorry," The Man said.

I hung my head to show that I was sorry too, about that and about my embarrassing display.

"We're thinking of getting another cat," The Editor said.

"But not right away," The Husband said.

"So," The Man said, in an awkward segue clearly designed to get us off the topic of dead cats. The Man swung his arms, bringing them together in a clap. "I guess I'm ready for my relationship tutorial!"

The Editor groaned and rolled his eyes, and I gotta say, I didn't blame him.

"Or," he countersuggested, "we could all sit down together, like normal people, and have polite conversation."

Dinner proved to be something vegetarian, so, not my favorite.

"Oh!" The Editor said. "Here!" Then he got out a can of what I knew to be very high-priced dog food. "It's beef stew," he informed me, opening the can. "We bought it for you today."

The Editor carried the bowl out to the dining room and set it down on the floor next to the seat I assumed was meant for The Man.

Wine was poured—none for me, thanks—and The Man looked at the ruby substance in his glass like it was foreign to him. "I, um . . ."

"Look," The Editor said, "if I have to drink beer at your place, you can drink wine here. Cheers!"

"Uh, cheers," The Man said, clinking glasses with The Editor.

"Mmm," The Husband said, "what a lovely Pinot."

"So," The Man said, digging into his dinner, as it occurred to me that he was beginning an awful lot of sentences with the word "so." "What do you do?" he asked The Husband.

"I'm a window washer."

"He's being modest," The Editor said. "He's a high-rise window washer."

"Sounds dangerous," The Man said.

"Don't get him started," The Husband said genially, indicating The Editor with his fork.

"Every time I hear one of those reports about window washers trapped on a scaffold that's malfunctioned, my heart is in my throat," The Editor said.

"It's no worse than me worrying that one of your authors will give you a heart attack."

The Man had the good grace to look ashamed at this, and I cast my eyes downward too. We could be a lot.

"Oh, not you," The Editor said kindly. "I deal with much worse than you."

Small potatoes, maybe, but we'd take it.

"So, how'd you get into window washing?" The Man asked.

"When I graduated from college," The Husband said, "it occurred to me that I had absolutely no interest in pursuing what I'd gone to college for. At the same time, it occurred to me that I liked being outdoors, I didn't mind heights, and I really liked windows." He shrugged. "Plus, all day long, my mind is my own."

"You two just seem, um, really different from each other."

"Different in some ways," The Husband said.

"But the same in others," The Editor said.

"I just don't really get it," The Man said. "Twenty-five years. You've been together for twenty-five years. I can't even imagine. How did you manage that?"

"We may seem different," The Editor said, "but we have a lot in common."

"We both love books," The Husband said.

"Not always the same ones, but it's enough to share the same general passion for something."

"So that's it?" The Man sounded equal parts perplexed and disappointed. "Having something in common? But that makes no sense. Because if that was the key to lasting successful relationships, almost everyone would be able to do it. And that's clearly not the case. Do you never fight about anything?"

"Oh, we fight," The Editor said.

"But we learned a long time ago," The Husband said, "that just because you can think of a perfect nasty comeback in your head, it doesn't necessarily have to find its way out of your mouth."

"So, you don't say what you really feel?" The Man said.

"We do," The Editor said.

"But we're careful about how we say it," The Husband said.

"No one needs to go in for the kill," The Editor said. "It's more important to communicate and think of the other person than to always be right."

"The most important and probably most difficult thing for two people to grasp when they move in together," The Husband said, "is that the other person isn't you."

"I don't follow," The Man said tensely. He was already starting to look overwhelmed. Hell, his upper lip was even perspiring.

"People often think they need to change the other person," The Editor said, "that their way of doing things is right and that if they can bend the other person to their will, they'll be happy. But that way madness lies."

"You're talking about compromise," The Man said. "The secret is learning to compromise?"

"No," The Husband said, "it's about learning to honor the differences in the other person, it's recognizing that you're each separate people and that that's OK, and that the two of you together is a third entity. You're not two pieces of a puzzle that make one whole. You have to acknowledge you're both whole already."

"Exactly," The Editor agreed, "honoring the differences. After twenty-five years, he still puts the toilet paper on the wrong way."

"Over."

"It's under."

"Over, over, over."

The Man looked between the two of them like the ball at a tennis match. Ooh, who wouldn't love a good *thwack thwack thwack*?

Well, The Man wouldn't, apparently. He wasn't doing so hot.

"Thank God we have two bathrooms here," The Editor said.

"I could probably learn to put the toilet paper on the other way," The Man offered. "I'm not completely inflexible."

"Not really the point," The Editor said. The Man bit his tongue, looked down at his food.

"Look," The Husband said, "every romantic relationship starts, hopefully, with great passion."

"But it's kindness," The Editor said, reaching across the table and taking his hand, "that always saves you in the end."

The Editor released The Husband's hand and took a swig of his wine before adding, "And you also might try bringing Gatz on a few less dates, if you want the relationship to have a chance at going the distance. You know: focus on her needs and not just your own."

While I never liked being left behind and always liked to go with, I could see where he had a point.

But when I looked across at The Man, it was obvious that, whatever I was seeing, The Man wasn't seeing it too. If anything, he looked more perplexed than ever. No doubt, he was still hung up on the toilet paper.

We had dessert, the conversation shifting to books, and The Man came up with an excuse to leave soon after that, at least remembering to thank our hosts. He even complimented the Pinot.

But as we made our way home, I realized just how perplexed he was—walking fast, his eyes racing—when he said, "I could never attain and maintain that level of perfection!"

That's what you took away from the evening? Dude, you are totally missing the point!

I trotted quickly alongside to keep up, my own furry upper lip beginning to perspire from the nerves The Man was giving me.

Chapter Nine

Really kinda wish I could quit October at this point!

It was late in the day and we were taking an über-romantic stroll in Hudson River Park, The Woman and New Man holding hands, her head against his shoulder. Me, I was content to be on a leash if it meant I could be with them and enjoy all the great views. But then I got so wrapped up in that and rubbernecking at passersby that it took me a beat to register that the mood had shifted.

"I'm not saying I wish you were suffering too," The Woman said, sounding uncharacteristically defensive. "I'm just saying, well, why *aren't* you suffering too?"

Apparently, the question Tall had raised, about why The Woman was the only one being attacked online when it takes two to tango and New Man had had an equal role in tangoing—not that they'd done anything unethical!—had clearly been festering inside The Woman ever since, and now that festering was finally coming home to roost.

New Man, to his credit, didn't take offense. Rather, he seemed to be carefully weighing how to say what he wanted to say next.

"I'm beginning to think," said New Man, "that maybe none of this has anything to do with the #MeToo movement after all."

"How can you say that?" said The Woman. "Of course it's about that."

"Well, of course. Not to be Captain Obvious, that's what they think they're fighting for." He paused, weighing his next words more carefully still. "But I don't think that has anything to do with the inciting incident. I don't think that's what was bothering the original poster. No matter what she says, it's got nothing to do with sexual exploitation and unequal power in the workplace and all the other things this has turned into, which are all very important issues, but those issues have nothing to do with this, with us."

"But if it's not about that, then what else could it be?"

Sometimes, you need to proceed with caution, dipping one toe in the water at a time, and other times, you need to jump right in, causing the water to splash wherever it may.

Apparently, we'd proceeded to the ripping-off-the-bandage portion of water immersion, and to heck with me worrying about mixing my metaphors all over the place.

"I think @SimplySimantha is my stalker," New Man said.

"*What*?"

The Woman had stopped strolling, shocked, and I was shocked too. We'd stopped strolling the path so abruptly, the people who'd been behind us briefly bumped into us before doing the "excuse me" thing and going around the roadblock we were creating.

What???

Back when The Woman and New Man were first getting to know each other, she had him over to Book Club, where, during the course of the night, he'd alluded to someone he referred to as his "stalker": a woman who sent him messages with far more frequency than the average fan; those messages sometimes veering into the creepy lane, like the time she got upset when he updated the author pic on his website. OK, so maybe that sounded a little . . . *off*; like, I may *prefer* Brad Pitt when his hair is a little shorter, but when it's longer, I'm not about to send the guy letters about it—it's his hair. And to think that someone who would do that kind of thing would jump the trolley into doing something like this, so destructive to someone else's career, seemed like a too-big leap. And yet . . .

It was getting dark and the streetlamps overhead winked on.

That's when the light bulb went on over my head.

Jealousy. Was there a bigger motive for a lot of human behavior?

The Woman must've had the same thought because I saw the dawning realization in her eyes.

"How long have you suspected this?" she said.

"Almost from the beginning."

"And you didn't think to tell me?"

"I guess I thought it was obvious. I saw no reason to be a captain about it."

"It wasn't obvious to me!"

He could've responded with heat of his own then. A lot of humans might've. But instead he closed the gap between them, gently cradled her elbows with his palms, and pulled her in close.

"I'm sorry," he said. "I guess I saw no point in hammering the point home, when what could be done about it? I didn't want to somehow make things worse."

"But that's information I should've had."

"You're right. I'm sorry."

"Maybe I'd have handled it differently, if I'd known that." But before he could apologize again, she said, "It's not your fault other people have turned it into something else. People turn things into something else all the time. This time I was just unlucky that people turning something into something else happened to happen to me."

"But it'll pass," he said, pulling her closer.

She settled in, a look of nerves passing quickly off her face.

They held each other for a time and then he tilted her chin up, lowering his lips to hers. They were individually such beautiful people, and together the combination of them was positively dazzling. It wasn't just me thinking that either; I could tell by all the "aws" coming from other strollers as they made their way around the kissing couple. Everyone could see how in love with each other they were.

There'd been some minor turbulence there, even a raised voice, but the storm had passed. At least for now.

Chapter Ten

I'm not even gonna say it this time . . .

There was a palpable sadness in the air. Ever since our dinner at The Editor and The Husband's place, The Man had grown convinced he was a failure.

"I'll never get it right," he said, sighing as he sprawled across his bed at three p.m. in his bathrobe. "I'll never win a woman like her."

Well, not with that negative attitude you won't, buddy.

I did my best to cheer him up.

Picking up his sneakers with my teeth and tugging them over to him one at a time, I dropped them at his feet, letting my tongue hang out while wagging my tail.

"The Bar?" he said. "I don't feel like The Bar tonight."

Aw, crap. But you used to like The Bar!

When Plan A fails, there's always Plan B.

Trotting over to the stereo system, I nudged at dials until (1) it was on and (2) I finally found a tune I liked.

Then I started thumping my tail to the beat and shaking my furry booty at the same time.

"I'm not in the mood for dancing, Gatz."

Aw, c'mon. You'll feel better! You like dancing!

"No, you're the one who likes dancing. I only do it for you."

You like it too. You just won't admit it. Once we get going, you'll get into it.

"Seriously, I'm not up for it."

Party pooper.

But then it occurred to me. If he was willing to sometimes dance with me to make me happy—and sometimes wound up enjoying himself in the process, in spite of himself—maybe he could go ahead and do something for New Woman, even if it was something he didn't normally like to do?

Going to the kitchen, I nosed open one of the below-counter cabinets and began pawing pots and pans out. These were items that did not typically see use by us, certainly not for their intended uses, The Man being more of a beer / box of cereal / frozen pizza / takeout food kind of guy.

"What are you doing, Gatz?" he asked with an annoyance he almost never directed at me, having managed to get out of bed to follow the source of the clattering into the kitchen.

I went over to him, stood on my hind legs, and nudged at the spot where I could tell his phone was in his pocket. Then I went back to the pots and pans and began nudging them closer to the stove.

He took his phone out of his pocket, looked at it, then looked at the pots and pans.

"I . . . I guess I could call her."

I thumped my tail.

"I could offer to make dinner for her tonight."

I thumped my tail again. Now we were cooking with gas! Women love it when you make dinner for them!

"I dunno . . . I'm no good in the kitchen."

Refusing to be defeated, even if he was, I returned to the open cabinet door, only this time, I crawled all the way inside, nosing around until I found what I wanted all the way in the back. Then I circled around it and pushed it forward until the colander clattered out onto the kitchen floor. He let out a smile and laughed at the ridiculousness of my choice of kitchenware.

"Spaghetti? You're saying I should offer to make her spaghetti?"

Yes! Everyone likes spaghetti! And anyone can make spaghetti because it's so easy. In fact, I'd do it for you myself, but I don't have opposable thumbs!

I expected him to raise even further objections, because he can be a bit like that, and I was prepared to wait him out. I was prepared to counter any objections that came my way. But I didn't have to, because a light had gone on in his eyes.

"You know, you're right—I can do this!"

Course you can! I've heard tell that if you can read, you can cook, and almost no one reads better than you!

I listened as he called to invite her, and he even sounded happy and excited while doing so. She must've said yes, because as soon as they hung up, he went to grab his keys from the handy hook by the door. I figured we were going out to get ingredients, and further figured I'd be going with him, because he'd need my help picking out all the right things, and because I love a good outing, but he had other ideas.

"I think," he said, "that this may call for more than I can get from the bodega that doesn't mind you shopping with me. I hope you understand."

I did understand. I may not have liked it, I may have hoped that someday dogs would be welcome everywhere, but I did understand, and I certainly didn't want to stand in the way of a chance at love.

Especially not after all the work I'd done getting that colander out.

So I licked his hand and barked my acceptance of the situation to let him know we were good.

"Thanks, Gatz." He grinned, patting me on the head, distracted but very excited. Before heading out the door, he began making a mental list of what to get. "Let's see . . . some kind of whole tomatoes, and pasta obviously, maybe some spices . . . flowers for the table . . . and wine too . . . ? She's beer and I'm beer, but sometimes people favor wine with their pasta . . ."

And he was gone, excited.

And I stayed, excited.

There was such a feeling of hope in the air now, and I wanted this for him so much, for him to have a romantic relationship that made him happy in the way The Woman's with New Man made her. And I was sure New Woman was The One to do it, so sure, I didn't mind that he left me alone for what seemed a lot longer than I thought it should take.

When he returned, he had all the items he'd mentally listed: flowers and sauce ingredients, spices and pasta; he'd even remembered the wine. But, once again, the mood had shifted. I could smell it on the air.

As he listlessly deposited the items on the counter, I went over to him, tugged on his pant leg, tried to convey my willingness to help out in any way I could. I'd find a way to help him cook, lack of opposable thumbs be damned!

But it was no use.

"It's no use, Gatz," he said, looking at all the items on the counter, overwhelmed. "What was I thinking? I'm no cook. I have no idea what I'm doing."

And then he phoned New Woman, told her not to bother coming, went back to bed, and that was that.

Chapter Eleven

Halloween!

Who cared if it was still October, the month of some conflict and heartache; it was Halloween!

And even better than that?

It was Take Your Child to Work Day at the publishing company where The Woman worked. Even though it was a weekday, The Woman had received a dispensation from The Man so she could have custody of me for the day, just for this special occasion.

I'd been to Take Your Child to Work Day at her place of business before, more than once, but it had never fallen on Halloween—what an amazing twofer!

I've always loved Halloween, the opportunity to see all kinds of people, especially little kids, arrayed in their costumes. Walking down the street, you never know what you're going to see, something incredibly cool or something incredibly odd—which in New York City could also happen on any day ending in a Y—but Halloween was like the normal city on steroids. For myself, my humans always knew not to try putting me in a costume. Clothes are for people, not dogs.

I'd also always loved Take Your Child to Work Day. The kids of all the employees—editors and art people and marketing and all the rest—always made a big fuss about me; really, I was always the hit of the day. Plus, publishing kids, in my experience, are great kids. Unlike occasional kids on the street who might grab and pet first and ask questions later, they always asked permission and I appreciated their respect for my bodily integrity.

So the idea of having both things occur at once—great kids! in great costumes!—was almost more joy than I could bear.

And what a Halloween morning it had proven to be! Lately it had been quite cold, more like the old days before climate change hit these parts, or so I'm told. But that day it was so beautiful, cloudless and warm, I doubted anyone would need to wear odious coats over their costumes once evening came.

We were running late, which was unlike The Woman, widely known for her punctuality. But that was OK by me. I figured maybe this year, she wanted us to be the last to arrive. You know, so I could make a grand entrance in all my furry glory.

As we entered the building and approached the security desk, there was still a line of people waiting to be admitted. Craning my neck so I could view the line, I hoped to see at least a few kids in costumes. Maybe there'd be a superheroine? Or a pirate—aargh, matey! But I didn't see any kids, just adults. Well, there were lots of other companies with offices in the building.

When we were at last at the desk, The Woman barely paused her step, greeting the guard with a hearty hello and a big smile while flashing her ID. It's what I'd seen her do every time I'd been there with her. The Woman was a big-cheese editor; everyone on the desk knew who she was; there was no need to stop her. And yet . . .

"Oh!" the guard said, putting his arm out in front of her, adding an awkward, "Hey, no. You can't go up yet."

"Excuse me?" The Woman said, but not in that entitled and imperious way a lot of people use those two words, like next thing you know they'll be demanding to see a manager. She was simply puzzled by something that had never happened before. Me, I was puzzled too.

"I just, um," the guard said, more awkward yet, "yeah, I'm supposed to call upstairs first."

Which he did.

"Someone will be down shortly," he said. "If you could, um, just step to one side here for now . . ."

Which we did.

And watched the parade of people who'd been piling up behind us pass by, some occasionally eyeing us up and down, wondering what we'd done wrong.

Nothing. We've done nothing wrong.

But apparently not everyone agreed because a few minutes later a bald man in a suit emerged from one of the elevators, striding straight for us.

I knew this bald guy. I'd met him on some of my previous visits to the building. He was The Publisher, The Woman's boss. One time, he told me he had a dog of his own at home. But I'd had my doubts. Some people, the way they talk about dogs, you can tell they're just making it up.

"I'm sorry," were the first words out of his mouth.

I was puzzled, but The Woman wasn't as I saw realization dawn in her eyes, which flashed with sadness, pain, and finally a touch of anger as her mouth settled into a grim line.

"I can't believe you're doing this," she said.

"It's out of my control," he said.

"It's in your control more than it is anyone else's."

"They've called for a boycott of our entire line of books now. They're threatening to go through with it if we don't do something about, and I quote, 'our unhealthy work environment.'"

"But it's not an unhealthy work environment. I did nothing wrong!"

To this he said nothing. It'd have been nice if he reassured her then, that it wasn't her fault; any decent human with a shred of chivalry would have at least done that. Maybe he was scared of her filing a lawsuit?

"We even went to HR in the beginning," she said, "before we started our relationship, even though he's not technically an employee of the company. We went to you too. You know I did nothing wrong!"

Again, to this he said nothing.

Oh, he was definitely worried about a lawsuit.

"Why won't you stand up for me?" she demanded to know. "Why are you giving in to the mob?"

"It's not just any mob. Of course, there are a few bad apples, but people are legitimately up in arms about abuses in the workplace."

"Yes, I know all that. But what about when they're wrong?"

He shrugged, sadly, but still a shrug.

"And I'm to be collateral damage?"

"Look, I know you hoped this would all blow over in time. We all did."

"So, you're firing me, then?"

"Oh, goodness, no!"

"You're not?" There was a glimmer of hope in her eyes. "I'm not fired?"

"Absolutely not." Pause. "It's best for all of us if you resign. And, if you think about it, that would be best for you too, in the long run. Of course, I'll be happy to give you a good letter of recommendation—glowing, even. And we'll be sure to have all your things couriered to you."

I waited for another "but" from her, at least one last fiery objection, but there were no more "buts" to be had.

Shock in her eyes, she turned on her heel. She began to tear up and looked over at the security guard with a soft smile. "Thank you for always making my mornings brighter." He smiled back at her in sympathy and nodded. We headed back to the revolving doors and out onto the street, each brisk step taking us farther and farther away from the building in which The Woman had worked since long before I met her. If it had been anyone else in her situation they would just crumble, but The Woman was the epitome of strength and grace, holding her head high as she walked away.

What a sucky Halloween, with all tricks and no treats.

As for The Publisher, I bet I'd been right about him all along. The spineless worm probably never even had a dog. I bet all he had was a goldfish.

Chapter Twelve

All Saints' Day . . .

You'd think that, after all my complaining, I'd be excited about it being a new month. But there were no saints to be had and, even if there were, when I was with The Man, we were a Jewish household, albeit nonpracticing.

Hey, I could still use "albeit" correctly in a sentence, so at least I still had that going for me.

As for The Man, he couldn't even write a correct sentence. Ever since his failed attempt to make dinner for New Woman—failed because there had been no real attempt on the making-dinner part, other than the gathering of provisions—he'd been in a lousy funk. If not the worst I'd ever seen him in, it was definitely a close contender.

So, there we were, lying on the couch in all our slothful lack of glory, him on his back, me draped across his midsection, my chin drooping gloomily over the side of his waist, when there came a knock at our door.

I looked at him; he looked at me; we both shrugged—neither of us could remember inviting anyone over.

He made no move to move me so he could get up and answer the door. As for me, I'd have been happy to do it for him. I'd do anything for that guy, if I could. But while I'd had success in the past opening doors, the lock had always proven a dexterity challenge too far.

Eh. Whoever it was would no doubt grow bored and go away.

But the knocking came again, louder and more insistent than the first time, impossible to ignore.

With a resigned sigh, The Man gently dislodged me from his stomach and made his meandering way to the door, me following along behind him. Normally, I'd be eager to see who was calling—even unsolicited solicitors could have their entertainment value—but listlessness can be as contagious as any other emotion, and we just weren't feeling it.

But you know who was feeling it?

New Woman.

Because no sooner had The Man unlatched the door than she blew in like a hurricane.

"What is *wrong* with you?" she stormed. "Ever since you invited me to dinner and then canceled, you don't answer my calls, you don't answer my texts . . . If you're trying to break up with me, at least have the courage to do it to my face, instead of leaving me to guess. How could you ghost me?"

"But I didn't ghost you."

"What do you call it, then? What is *wrong* with you?" She stopped suddenly, hands on hips, and surveyed the room. "And what the *hell* is wrong with this place?"

For the first time in days, I saw our surroundings through fresh eyes: a week's worth of empty beer cans strewn across the coffee table, the stacks of empty takeout pizza boxes, discarded socks on the floor—at least he was still putting on fresh socks every day, with my encouragement—and the stack of manuscript pages beside the laptop, the ones The Editor had dropped off weeks ago, which were silently screaming in their Munchian fashion: *untouched*.

Yes, I'd been down this road before with The Man, but never quite this far down it.

"Oh no," she said, hand to mouth. "Not you too."

"Not me too what?"

"You suffer from depression, don't you?"

The Man started to deny it, but his hair, without the usual Mets cap to cover it, told a different story. He should've showered that morning. Even a shower within the past four days might've helped.

"Don't even try to deny it," she said. "How long has this been going on? What precipitated it?"

At first, he seemed to be confused by the question. What started it? When he got depressed, he didn't see there being an identifiable event. But as he verbally backtracked through the last few weeks—this week's slide, the failed attempt at dinner with her, dinner with The Editor, The Editor bringing unexpected revision notes, our dinner at her place with her and Hoops when she'd said he'd need to court her . . .

"Oh no!" she gasped. "It's my fault!"

"How can you think that? It's no one's fault, except mine, maybe. This just happens sometimes."

"Yes, but I had no idea you'd take my remarks about you needing to court me so hard, I had no idea you'd be overwhelmed by them, and I certainly had no idea you suffer from depression."

"But I don't suffer from depression."

"Don't be ridiculous. That's like someone with an alcohol addiction insisting 'But I'm not an alcoholic.'"

I could see him trying to rouse himself to object further, but she was on a roll.

"Take those pages your editor brought you, for instance," she said, going over and tapping her finger against the top one. "Normally, you'd get revision notes and your first reaction would be to rant and rave to yourself about how wrong your editor is; you'd swear at your computer; you'd tell yourself your pages were fine as they are."

"How did you know I do that?"

"Because *I* do that. *All* writers do that. But then, after anywhere from five minutes of ranting to five days of quietly fuming, you'd feel your blood pressure return to normal; you'd look at the notes again but this time with an objective eye, an *editorial* eye. You'd assess the situation, come to agreement with the notes where the notes were right, which would likely be ninety to one hundred percent of the time, and you'd get down to the business of fixing everything that needed fixing, to the best of your ability."

Slowly, he nodded.

"But this time?" she said. "No, no, no, no, no. You became completely engulfed by those notes; even the very idea of them presented to you a tsunami you were sure you'd never be able to swim out from under, so you've done nothing with them at all, probably haven't even looked at them."

Reluctantly, he nodded in agreement.

"And this place!" she remarked again, throwing her arms up. "I bet you get up in the morning, you come out here, if you've in fact slept in your bedroom and aren't just permanently installed on the couch. The first thing you see is the mess, and you think, 'I should really do something about this. How would it look if someone unexpected stopped by? And even if I don't care about that, even if I don't care about myself, shouldn't I make this place nicer for Gatz?'"

I looked up at him, noting his resigned agreement as he looked down at his feet on the carpet. Maybe she had a point.

"But you just can't do it," New Woman went on. "You think about starting with one can, but you know that won't really do anything; you can't see that that would at least get the process reversed and moving in the right direction; all you can see is the enormity of the task before you, and, like with the manuscript, it is simply too much. So what do you do? Nothing at all. As things get worse and even worse. And you wait. Until one day, the sun looks like something resembling the bright orb it used to be before it transformed into a pale substitute. When that happens, you can start to clean up; you can start doing the work of being a writer again."

By this point, he was gaping at her, as was I, tongue out and all, on my part.

"How do you know all that?" he asked incredulous.

She sighed, exasperated. "Because! *I* suffer from depression too!"

The Man appeared dumbfounded. "You suffer from depression?"

I could relate to those doubts. Yes, we'd all thought they were mirror images of each other—antipathy to public appearances, fondness for flannel, love for the Mets and yadda yadda—but no one seeing the energetic dervish she was since she'd walked in could picture her as someone who could suffer from depression.

"Yeah, I do," she said. "All of these things you do—putting off work, putting off cleaning, putting off life because everything has suddenly become insurmountable—when the darkness comes, I do these things too."

"But right now you're good?"

She cast her eyes up, considering, as she seemed to take her own emotional temperature, before concluding with a nod, "Yeah, you know? Right now, I'm doing pretty OK."

"I'd say so," The Man said, with the first thing resembling a smile in many a day. It was a little wisp of a thing, gone as quickly as it came, but I'd seen it. And in that wisp of a smile, there was real admiration for her.

"But it won't last forever," she said. "The feeling good, or even just pretty OK, won't last forever for me, just like it never lasts for you. And then the darkness will roll back in again. When that happens? At least in my experience? You can't go over or under or around it; you've got to go through it, however long that takes."

"I've never met another person before," he said with a hint of wonder, "who could articulate what I feel."

She approached him then, raising her hands next to his cheeks but stopping before contact was made. "May I?" she asked gently.

With a nod, he closed his eyes and gratefully let his face make contact with her human touch.

"I think," she said, "we should try therapy."

That snapped his eyes back open.

Mine too.

"Joint therapy?" he said.

"Of course not!" she said, dropping his face.

"What are you talking about, then?"

Even to my ears, that sounded unwarrantedly argumentative. Thankfully, she didn't take it that way.

"Have you ever even tried therapy?" she asked.

He shook his head.

"Look, I'm sorry that what I said about you needing to court me precipitated the downward spiral into a depressed event."

He one-eye squinted at her. "So you're saying if we continued seeing each other, I *wouldn't* have to court you after all?"

"That is so not what I am saying. How can you be so thick?" She sighed, not a disgusted sigh, which could've been a death knell at that point, but rather, a relenting one. "Look, I like you. Who knows? I may even . . . more than like you."

He was listening, attentively listening.

"But that would never work," she said, "both of us living under the same roof, with both of us being the way we are. The only reason this is working right now"—she waved her finger back and forth between them—"is because we're not both down at the same time. But if we were under the same roof and both down at the same time? There'd be no saving us."

"So you're proposing . . ."

"You find a therapist and I find a therapist, preferably not the same one so no one feels weird about it."

"And then?"

"Then we'll see where we are. But at least we'll both be doing something we should've each been doing a long time ago, trying to live a better existence."

"And the courting?"

"I can wait a bit for that. Not forever, but I can wait a little longer. But you know what I can't wait longer for?"

He shook his head.

"This place! OK, here's what's going to happen. I'm going to start cleaning up and putting things away. If you're not feeling up to helping, that's OK, but at least when you get up tomorrow, you'll feel better when you come out here and your environment has been improved. Who knows? Maybe I'll need you to return the favor someday. Hopefully, though, you'll begin to feel guilty watching me clean your place and that guilt will drive you to start helping yourself. That's the theory anyway." She went on tiptoe to give him a quick peck on the forehead, and then the pizza box removal commenced.

"She's actually something, isn't she, Gatz?" he said. Then he picked up one of the empty beer cans and headed toward the kitchen.

Wanting to help the healing process begin, I knocked an empty can off the coffee table and began rolling my cleanup contribution toward the kitchen.

Obviously, it was a good thing that The Man and New Woman were going to individually go into therapy. But watching the two of them clean together, an odd mix of hope and melancholy in the air, a part of me couldn't help but think: If he suffered from depression and she suffered from depression, if The Woman had "resigned" from her job, and who knew what kind of fallout that might result in for her and New Man, were there to be no happy families anymore?

Chapter Thirteen

Book Club!

For the first time, there was to be no discussion of books at Book Club that evening, and no New Man this time either, because he'd decided to make himself scarce.

"You know how much I love putting nachos on a plate for you," he'd said earlier.

"And I love having you put nachos on a plate for me," she'd said.

"I live to put the right spoons in your fruit bowl."

"Mmm." She let out a low moan. "No one has ever put spoons in my bowl better. But . . ."

One long make-out session in the doorway later, and he was gone.

"I think I just need some quality time with my friends, you know?" The Woman explained to me. "And he gets that."

People getting things in a relationship is always a good thing, I'd come to learn. Having all the passion in the world is one thing, but if there's no understanding to accompany it, no really seeing the other person and what they need, how far is that going to take you?

The doorman called up to say our guests had arrived, and soon thereafter, The Blonde, The Redhead, and The Brunette were making their way off the penthouse elevator, each with a bottle of wine in hand. They don't usually all come thus armed, so I figured it was going to be that kind of night.

I knew The Woman hadn't seen them since the firing that turned out to be a resignation but really was, for all intents and purposes, a firing. But as they trooped in, one after the other, rather than the usual squeals of "Gatz!" as they greeted me, instead each gave me sad, consoling pats on the head accompanied by mournfully muted utterances of "Gatz."

And when they greeted The Woman, it was in the same way, with wistful hugs and murmurings of "I'm so sorry it went down that way."

Which was when The Woman broke into peals of laughter, exclaiming, "What is wrong with everyone? This isn't some kind of funeral—it's an opportunity!"

That's when I realized just how OK everything was, contrary to some recent assumptions I'd been making about us. We were like Mark Twain that way: the reports of our demise had been greatly exaggerated. Well, he was dead now, but he wasn't the first time people thought he was.

Still, despite her upbeat words, and my upbeat reaction to them, it quickly became apparent that the others weren't taking it the same way. She smiled brightly and began to flit around the space. "Can I get you guys anything? I have tea—green tea, black tea, chamomile tea . . ."

The three looked at one another nervously.

"You don't need to put on a brave face for us," The Redhead said.

"I know that if I were in your situation," said The Blonde, "I'd be going back and forth between livid and sad so often, I'd make myself emotionally dizzy."

"If you think it would be any comfort," The Brunette said, covering The Woman's hand with her own, "I'd be willing to lend you Sparky." Sparky was the pet snake, I presumed. She eyed me in consideration before adding, "I think Gatz is big enough, so you don't have to worry about Sparky eating him." And finally: "Oh, hey!

Where do you keep the wine opener?" She said this while waving her bottle in the air, which, it's worth pointing out, had a twist-off cap.

But the other bottles didn't, and as The Woman led them all toward the kitchen, she threw over her shoulder, "I appreciate the offers of commiseration and a snake, but really, I'm fine!"

See, ladies? She's fine!

"But you're not fine," said The Blonde.

"You can't be," said The Redhead.

"Why can't I be?" said The Woman.

"Because no one would be fine with this," the Redhead said. "Because I wouldn't have been fine with this."

"And that's what makes the world go round," The Woman said, laughing, "different people reacting differently to different things!"

She got out the corkscrew and began opening the bottles they'd brought that needed one, uncapped The Brunette's bottle, and, for good measure, removed a fourth bottle from the special wine refrigerator and opened that as well. Usually, they just go one bottle at a time. Apparently tonight there were going to be choices.

Then she got out four glasses and everyone poured what they wanted. Me, I went over to my water dish and took a quick slurp, just to be part of the gang and, you know, show some solidarity. I trotted back to the group in time to see The Woman pouring herself a full glass, the others eyeing her carefully as the red made its way to the brim. She sipped the edge so it wouldn't spill over and pulled bags of various chips out of cabinets, pouring their contents into bowls.

Prior to the guests arriving, I'd noticed the lack of telltale odors in the air that were always a prelude to Book Club; you know, hors d'oeuvres. But as everyone grabbed their own glasses and a bowl, following The Woman out to the living room, I realized it was going to be Chips in a Bowl Entertaining, which was more like the kind of entertaining The Man typically did, only in his case, there would've only been one bag and no bowl, his hand digging into the bag for a handful before passing it around.

Everyone settled into the couch; drinks were drunk; chips were munched.

"We should've come sooner," The Blonde offered quickly as The Woman took another sip.

"We would've come sooner," The Redhead mentioned. "But we thought you might need some space."

"Exactly," The Brunette said. "Like whenever Sparky eats a mouse? He needs some space afterward to digest it. In fact, it's a couple of weeks before he's ready to eat again."

"You realize that's the worst analogy ever?" The Blonde sighed. "It has nothing to do with the situation at hand."

The Brunette opened her mouth, let out a small "But—"

"I know you all mean well," The Woman said, smiling widely, "and I can't tell you how much I appreciate it, but your concern is unnecessary. I'm fine!" she exclaimed, taking a long sip of her drink. The three friends eyed one another nervously as The Woman gulped down the rest.

"We could've quit too," The Blonde said, as though The Woman hadn't spoken at all.

It occurred to me then that you can tell people something, like The Woman saying she was fine, and you could even repeat the same thing over and over again, but those people were still going to hear what they wanted or expected to hear.

How rude, I thought to myself. *Couldn't these people see she was fine?*

"I'm fine," The Woman asserted, escaping the relentless group to the kitchen island.

"We should've just quit." The Redhead got up to follow her, the other two in tow. "We were so angry on your behalf."

"We really should've," The Brunette said. "We should've shown, you know, solidarity."

And that's one of the reasons I love these women, dotty though they may sometimes be. They believe in solidarity, and the Gatzer is about nothing if it's not solidarity with his people.

"You know," The Blonde said, "we could still quit—"

"*STOP!*" The Woman cried.

Well, they heard her that time. The three froze, stunned, and The Woman sighed.

"Look," she said in a softer voice, "I've said I'm fine with it, I don't know how many different times and ways I can find to tell you that, and I am."

"But how can you be fine with it?" The Brunette said, perplexed.

Look at her! She's The Woman! Of course she's fine!

"Because, as much as I hate the phrase most of the time, 'it is what it is,'" The Woman said. "It's over with, done. What good does it do me to dwell on it? What good would it do me if you lost your jobs as well? I don't want that. Nothing about that would make me happy. Nothing about that would make this better. I just got unlucky. But there's no reason anyone else should suffer for it too."

"But aren't you mad at him?" The Blond said.

"Not even a little bit?" The Redhead said.

"Who?" The Woman said. "The publisher? Of course, it would've been nicer if he'd shown a little more spine." She shrugged. "But I do get that he felt himself to be in an untenable position."

"No, not him," The Brunette said. Then she lowered her voice and jutted her chin toward various areas of the penthouse as she whispered, "*Him.*"

Ohhhh.

"Oh," The Woman said, both of us clearly twigging at the same time. They were talking about New Man. "Yeah, uh, no."

"I would be," The Blonde said.

"Doesn't it bother you," The Brunette said, "that he got out of this unscathed?"

"You know," The Woman said reflectively, "I thought about it, but I decided it's ridiculous. What good does it do for more people to suffer over this?"

And then, before The Brunette could push back again, which she was clearly gearing up to do, The Woman said, "I said this was an opportunity for me and I meant it. You know, I've worked at the same publishing company for my whole adult career. And while I've loved almost every minute of it, who's to say I can't find similar happiness, or even more happiness, at a different house?"

I certainly wasn't going to tell her differently. When she and The Man had broken up, I'd done my darnedest to bring them back together, to where I thought they'd been happiest, but then I'd realized she'd found even greater happiness with New Man.

It was, indeed, possible for people to go on to bigger and better-for-them things.

And if people say that living well is the best revenge, well, landing an even better publishing job had to rank right up there too.

"I haven't updated my résumé in years, though," The Woman said. "Who's up for helping me?"

So that's how we spent the rest of the evening, not complaining about the state of affairs and things that couldn't be changed, but rather, helping The Woman put together a new résumé so she could move forward.

We were all about solidarity.

Chapter Fourteen

Still November, but not in a bad way

Every dog has its day.

Nope, I didn't make that one up. Shakespeare didn't either, although that would be a good second guess. His version is slightly different and has a "hath" in there somewhere. There are, in fact, several versions of the sentiment, but the original seems to be from Queen Elizabeth I.

Anyway, it's a useful phrase to know and basically means the lowest or unluckiest will get their turn at some point, at least once.

This is by way of saying that The Man, who had been pretty low for some time, was finally having a day.

Or an evening, to be exact.

But before the dog could have his day or The Man could have his evening, there was a certain appointment that needed attending. An appointment with a therapist. I'd naturally assumed he'd want me to go with, but when I moved to follow him out the door, he told me this was one he had to do on his own. But at least The Man told me all about it when he got home.

Picture a large, round room with bay windows that let the sunlight shine into the space. Picture soothing blue walls and plush white chairs. Picture a dark hardwood floor, hanging plants, a furry area rug that would go great with a certain furry dog rubbing his back all over it. And finally, across from The Therapist—a woman of forty whose no-nonsense demeanor fit the job description well—was a certain male fella who couldn't stop bouncing his knee.

"What brings you in today?" She smiled, cracking open the Coke on her side table and taking a loud sip.

God, I could hear The Man thinking, *I can barely hear the construction outside.*

"Well, my, uh, my girlfriend wanted me to come in," he shared, tight-lipped.

The Therapist looked him up and down and nodded slowly. She placed her Coke carefully on the table and leaned forward, keeping her eyes on his. "Why'd she want you to come in?"

"Well, uh . . ."

The Therapist slowly looked down at his tapping foot. The Man quickly threw his one leg over the other, crossing them to stop the tapping. She continued to watch him. Then he switched the legs, throwing the other leg over the original leg, and seemed content with this decision. Until he uncrossed them. And resumed his tapping. The Therapist sat back in her chair, keeping her eyes on his. He cleared his throat loudly.

"I've been a little out of sorts lately, you could say, and she wanted me to meet with someone," he let out in one big breath, satisfied at finally getting that out.

"What's had you down?"

"*Oh my G*— Is it hot in here? I'm very . . . perspired."

She took her time to glance over at the thermostat to her right. "It's seventy degrees in this room."

"Right."

And for the most part, much of the session went like this. She tried to ask him what had bothered him; he tried to act as if nothing was wrong. She tried to indirectly ask him about his life; he got defensive and claimed those things were private. Finally, she asked him about his girlfriend, what she was like, what she did for a living, and The Man claimed she was over the line.

I mean, come on, dude—if you're going to pay the ridiculous amount you are likely paying to be sitting in this room with this professional lady, why are you dithering?

"We could play it your way," she finally said. "We don't need to talk about anything. In fact, you don't need to come here at all." She picked up her soda and took a loud sip. The Man nearly burst out of his chair from anxious foot tapping. She put it down and looked at him. "But you came here for a reason today."

The Man shifted in his chair and looked at The Therapist. He sighed.

"So." She crushed her Coke can in her hand and tossed it into the garbage can across the room before turning back to The Man. "What's had you down?"

"I . . . couldn't make my girlfriend dinner."

"Huh. OK . . . and why couldn't you make your girlfriend dinner?"

"Because I was depressed."

"Do you get depressed frequently?"

"Uh . . . it's been known to happen from time to time."

"And this time, why were you depressed?"

He took his time. Switched his legs around a few more times. Let out some lengthy sighs. To The Therapist's credit, she sat. She sat and waited.

"I went to my editor's apartment the other week so that he could teach me how to be good at relationships. And since I went, I've been upset because I'm not good at relationships. And that's what happened."

She nodded, waiting for him to offer more. He didn't.

"Why do you think you're bad at relationships?"

"Well, I think I'm bad at them because I have been bad at them and therefore, I know I'm bad at them—"

"Okay, you say that you've been bad at them in the past. How do you know that?"

"I got dumped."

"Why were you dumped?"

The Man sat back and gave this question serious consideration. I could imagine him thinking about The Woman and their relationship and the night they went dancing and ended things for real. And finally, he spoke. "We were wrong for each other. I thought the problem was that I wasn't willing to be the person she wanted; I wasn't willing to make compromises. She was more extroverted. I am, well, I'm introverted, definitely, I guess. And she loved to go out, she loved to be with people, and I couldn't do it. I was so stuck in my ways. And she didn't want to change me. So, we broke up."

"Is this a problem with the new girlfriend?"

"No . . . well, maybe . . . kind of. She's not like my ex; she's different."

"In what ways is she different?"

"She's . . . she's more like me. She doesn't exactly love industry parties. But maybe . . . I don't know. Maybe it's still a problem with her, too. But it's not like she wants me to completely change who I am."

"And you shouldn't. Perhaps it would be good practice for you, though, to say yes more often. You shouldn't become a different person for this woman, but if she mentions something that means a lot to her, maybe you could try it out. For her, and ultimately for yourself."

The Man leaned back in the chair, his legs calm for the first time since he sat down, with the light from the windows reflecting in his eyes. "Huh. Interesting."

She leaned back in her own chair and waited for him to speak again. Instead, he cast his eyes over to the clock on the wall. He hopped up and grabbed his jacket from behind him. "Well, guess it's quitting time!"

She glanced at the clock herself. "We still have ten minutes left . . ."

"I wouldn't want to waste your time—thank you, doc, perfect advice." He tried to push past her, but she stood up and blocked his path.

"OK. We can end early. But you mentioned that you've been depressed at multiple points throughout your life. Dealing with that . . . it can't be fixed in one session. We can work on it, though, together, so that you don't have to experience that as much."

He nodded quickly, not particularly listening. "Right, right. OK. Cool."

"Give me a call if you want to schedule a regular appointment—"

"Great—"

"—or let me know if you'd like a different therapist, and I can recommend a few colleagues for you—"

"Cool, cool, cool, sounds great."

She nodded at him sadly and stepped aside. He passed her and headed out the door. "Thank you!" he called. And he was gone.

But he returned home energized. He had an idea.

The Man had invited New Woman over for dinner, again, and this time he hadn't called back afterward to uninvite her. This time, the two of them were in the kitchen, cooking together. Well, actually, she was teaching him how.

"I can't believe you've never made yourself pasta with anything other than sauce in a jar," she said. "It's not hard to find recipes to make your own like this. You do know that if you can read, you can cook, right?"

See? That's what I'd been trying to tell him!

"That's OK, though," she said. "You'll learn. Now, first . . ."

Before I knew it, things were getting sautéed and tossed and all kinds of stuff was going on in that kitchen.

And before much longer, steaming plates of pasta were being brought out to the little table by the window, and The Man was asking her if she wanted some of the wine he'd brought for the previous dinner that hadn't happened.

"Are you crazy?" she said. "You know I drink beer."

"Yes, but I was just trying to be . . . thoughtful?"

"If you can't drink beer with it, why eat it?" she said. "You should at least know that about me by now."

They both had beers and he seemed pretty happy about that. Whatever changes he might be called upon to make down the road, at least he wasn't going to be called on to be "a wine guy."

Now, I'm not saying that he'd gone from being in the throes of depression to being some kind of devil-may-care slaphappy guy. And, in fact, the first part of the dinner convo was a bit solemn.

I kept forgetting that New Woman knew The Woman, that New Woman was one of her authors. Used to be.

"I can't believe they did that to her," New Woman said.

"Me neither," The Man agreed.

I knew he felt really bad about what had happened. And even though they were no longer together, I knew he wished he could do something to help make things better for her, somehow.

"And I hate to be totally self-absorbed about it," New Woman said, "but I don't know what I'm going to do without her. She was my editor, the *only* editor I've ever had; she knew how to talk to me; she knew how to talk me down from the ledge; she held my hand every step of the way. I'm not even sure who I'll be as a writer without her, or if I'll even still be any kind of writer at all."

"Of course you will," he said, "but I do get it. You know, when she and I were, um, together, she was always great about helping me with that stuff too. And then there's my own editor, who, no matter how much I complain, I don't know what I'd do without him either."

"She'll land on her feet. She's too good not to."

"And you'll figure out how to be a writer without her. It'll just take time."

After a brief moment of silence, New Woman said to The Man, a twinkle in her eye, "So, how was therapy?"

The Man forced a cheeky smile. "Apparently, I hate my mother!"

"Seriously?" New Woman laughed almost uncontrollably at this, barely able to sputter out the words, "And I love mine too much, and I obsess about what she thinks of me!"

At this, there were high-fives and high-paws all around.

So, maybe there was a slaphappy moment after all.

Chapter Fifteen

Still November . . .

Even though The Woman had told her pals at Book Club that she was fine, I'd come to realize she was putting on a brave face. On the inside, she was rattled. Who wouldn't be, though? Getting fired, even if you've been allowed to make it look like a resignation, is a traumatic event. No one likes being rejected, and discovering you can no longer work at the place you loved had to feel like an extra-big rejection. I do know her so well.

So again, while she'd made it seem to the others like she was ready to pound the pavement and get a new job instantly, it had taken her some time to pick herself up off the floor enough to get her mojo back.

But The Woman is nothing if not resilient, and by midday Sunday, she was ready to get going. There was just one problem.

New Man had an event, and she'd promised him that we'd definitely be at this one to lend moral support.

As we entered the room where it was to be held, I marveled at how many events this guy seemed to do . . . and all so well attended! The place was packed to the rafters, people so excited to see him in person, to hear him speak and get their books signed, no one was even paying attention to the coffee and cookies that had been set out.

The room immediately hushed all the buzzing as New Man

started to speak, and it occurred to me how much The Man would hate all this. And yet New Man was so smooth with it all, it was like breathing for him.

The crowd fed off his gracious composure, laughing in all the right spots and letting out a collective sighing "aw" whenever the talk turned moving.

"He's just so good at this, Gatz," she whispered to me, clearly proud.

But then the speech-making part of the event was over, people were applauding wildly, and it was time for schmoozing, to be followed by book signing.

We started to move forward to join the schmoozers, and of course The Woman would want to congratulate him on another successful event and kiss him, but then we saw that among the many people surrounding New Man stood The Publisher.

"I can do this, Gatz," she said as we inched forward in the throng.

Sure we can. We're tough.

"I have as much right to be here as anyone else. I can do this."

Of course we can!

"I can't do this. It's too soon. It's all too . . . *raw*."

The Woman pulled out her phone, texted New Man a reason why we had to leave early, and we were out of there. Well, who could blame her? As bad as losing her job had been, the afternoon had only served to exacerbate the damage: seeing how perfectly successful New Man still was while her own career had been destroyed, and the adding-insult-to-injury part of having the one who'd pulled the trigger on her, the Publisher, be there in such smiling proximity to New Man.

Back at the penthouse, she firmly decided to do something about her situation. But then her firmness started to waver.

"It's Sunday, Gatz," she told me as she sat on the couch with her laptop. "And while there are actually quite a few editorial openings on the publishing job boards that I could email my résumé to, jobs I think I'd be perfect for, it is Sunday."

I sat beside her on my haunches, eager to be of assistance, but I gotta admit: I had nothing. I couldn't see what the problem was.

"The thing is," she explained, "while I know that *technically* it doesn't matter whether I send it out on Sunday night or Monday morning, because whoever receives it will read it at the same time when they open their work email tomorrow, regardless, it's the psychology of the thing."

Still not getting it here.

"It's like this. If I push send on it now, even though I know it won't get opened until tomorrow, with each hour that passes, I'll start feeling more negatively about it. It will feel increasingly like a rejection, like I'm unwanted."

I'm getting it now! It's the psychology of the thing!

"And by the time I go to bed, I'll feel horrible, worse than ever. I might not even be able to sleep; that's how bad I'll feel."

If I know her well, it certainly sounded like she knew herself well too.

"But if I wait until first thing tomorrow morning to send it places . . ."

Then you can be reasonably happy tonight, get a decent night's sleep, and only have to endure the anxiety of waiting for responses for a far shorter period of time. I get it! But also? Aren't you going to get the intercom? It sounds like the doorman is buzzing us.

"Oops!"

She got up, crossed to the intercom, and talked to the doorman, and a few minutes later, The Man arrived. He was there to pick me up for the week.

After the usual exchange of pleasantries, The Man expressed again his sorrow and sympathies about what had happened.

"It just doesn't seem fair," he finished.

"Oh, well, fair." She laughed. "It's such a relative concept. Anyway, I've updated my résumé, and I'm ready to hit the metaphorical pavement tomorrow." To punctuate that last bit, she raised one arm and with a clenched fist made a gung ho gesture. This looked nervous on her, forced, and he nodded along.

"That's really great," he said. "Any publishing house would be lucky to have you."

"Thanks for that."

He looked around the room, which wasn't as tidy as it usually was; took in the state of her, also not as tidy. Then he put one finger to his lower lip as though a thought had just occurred to him.

"Oh, hey, I don't know why I didn't think of this earlier." And to illustrate just how deficient he found his own brain to be on whatever this matter was that had just occurred to him, he slapped himself on the head, like: *How stupid am I?*

"It's that," he went on, "well, I'm going to be out and about a lot this week."

"You," she deadpanned. "Out and about. A lot, no less."

Who did he think was buying this?

"It has been known to happen," he offered.

No, it hasn't.

"Anyway," he said, ignoring the heavy air of skepticism that had overtaken the room, "I know you're probably going to be busy going on a million interviews this week, but even though I'm supposed to have custody of Gatz on Monday through Friday, it'd be an enormous favor to me if you kept him this week."

"You could have called me and told me on the phone."

"I guess I, um, just remembered. You know, how busy I'm going to be."

"Right. So I'd get to keep Gatz for five more days?"

He nodded. She broke out into a smile, a bigger smile than I'd seen her muster all weekend.

"And then, what—you'd get him back on the weekend? The reverse of what we normally do?"

The Man shrugged. "That part doesn't matter right now. The important thing, I think, is that you keep Gatz for at least the next five days. You know, as a big favor to me."

"Because you'll be so busy with all your out-and-about things," she said softly.

"Exactly. Because I'll be so busy."

"Thank you," she said, more softly still, tears in her eyes.

"Anytime," he said, and then he took her in his arms, hugged her tight. "Um, I meant to say, no. Thank *you*. You know, for agreeing to take Gatz, so that I can . . ."

"I know exactly what you meant," she said in a muffled voice into his chest.

We all got it by now.

Even though they were no longer a couple, would never be a couple again, he still cared about her. He cared about her so much that even though he was going through his own difficult time, he'd rather go without me than have her go without me, if he thought she needed me more.

Odd as it sounds, I kind of wished New Woman could be there right then, so she could see what a wonderful and generous guy he could be, how he was capable of putting others before himself. It was the kind of moment that proved he was worth falling in love with.

They broke their embrace, her dabbing at the inside corners of her eyes with her index fingers.

"But will you be OK without him?" she asked, concerned.

"Of course."

"How have you been? How selfish of me, I haven't even asked you."

"I've been good." He forced a smile that looked convincing enough, but those in the know could tell there was still pain behind his eyes. He quickly crouched down beside me to avoid her eyes, ruffling the fur on my head.

"Be a good boy for her this week." He smiled at me.

As if I needed to be told to be a good boy. As if.

Then he put his head close to mine and whispered in my ear, "Take good care of her for me, Gatz."

Then he rose to his feet and was gone.

I tried to be a good boy for her.

I tried to take good care of her.

But sometimes when intentions meet up with reality, it's like two Porsches heading in opposite directions.

Take Monday, for instance.

After pushing send on all those résumés, she turned to me with a smile.

"You know what, Gatz?"

I looked up at her eagerly.

"Even though I know no one's likely to answer immediately, I might as well be prepared, just in case someone wants to interview me today."

With that, she changed out of her around-the-house pajamas and slippers and *hygge* stuff and into her best Working Woman Suit. She even put on makeup and heels.

But no one emailed back. No one asked her to come in.

Tuesday, she sent follow-up emails and got dressed up again.

She studied her fingernails. "Perhaps I should touch up my manicure?"

But the manicure created no hiring magic. We were still getting no response.

Wednesday, dressed and manicured, she started making phone calls.

"If I can just talk to a human being, I know I can persuade someone to hire me."

But no one would take her call.

Thursday, she started sending her résumé to small publishers that were so small, she hadn't even heard of them before.

"Last Hope Press?" she said. "Sounds about right, so I might as well."

In fact, it was some kind person at Last Hope Press who did finally call her on Friday morning.

The Woman was so excited to get the call that she put it on speakerphone so I could hear too.

"I'm really sorry," the voice came through, so hushed, I felt like we were suddenly in the middle of a spy film. "I shouldn't even be calling, but I felt like someone should tell you. While we'd normally kill to get an editor of your caliber here and any publisher should be happy to have you, we won't be able to offer you a job right now. You're simply too hot to touch. I hope you understand."

And then they hung up.

We'd been blackballed.

Where was New Man during all this? He'd been mostly lying low, trying to be sensitive to The Woman's need to just handle this all herself, but he'd pop in to provide support whenever that was needed too.

"It's so wrong," he said, massaging her shoulders.

"I bet if I had a different name," she said, "I could get a job like that." She snapped her fingers.

Then, to prove her point, she made up a new email account, changed the name on her résumé while keeping everything else the same, and sent it to the most prestigious house looking for an editor.

Almost instantly, she got a reply, asking when would it be convenient for her to come in for a job interview.

"Are you going to really do that?" New Man said. "Are you going to take a job under an assumed identity?"

"Of course not," she said, deleting the publisher's reply in disgust. "I'm not some character on a TV show. Besides, did they really believe Jane Doe was applying for a job?"

We all shared a good chuckle over that one.

"I'm not going to resort to changing my name," she said resolutely. "I am who I am."

Damn straight. She was The Woman.

"So what are you going to do?"

It was almost as if she hadn't heard him. She was tapping a pen on the table, deep in thought, over and over and over again.

Chapter Sixteen

Still November!

The Man and I were stretched out across his bed in the middle of the day, doing some quality male bonding, when the front door slammed and New Woman stormed in, waving a text from The Man in the air. "What do you mean you don't do anything for Thanksgiving?" New Woman demanded.

Yes, Thanksgiving was fast approaching. And no, The Man never really did anything for that holiday. Or any other holiday, really. If he remembered to buy someone a heart-shaped box on Valentine's Day, that was pretty big for him. Oh, but he always celebrated my birthday, Real and Official: Real was the day he adopted me in February, because he didn't really know when I was born, and Official was the first really great day in June so we could celebrate outside.

But other than that?

It was holidays that finally broke The Man and The Woman up the previous year. The first Hanukkah/Christmas season they were together, they celebrated both quite happily, and we even went to see her family for Christmas, which was uncomfortable for him, but fun for her and me. Second year they were together, she persuaded him to go see his parents on Hanukkah, which was a disaster. The third year, he didn't want to go anywhere. He'd had enough. And then she'd had enough too.

As for the three Thanksgivings they'd been together, somehow The Woman hadn't minded taking just me to see her family, since (1) he'd always say he needed to write and she respected that; (2) she and her family are British, and while she's now a US citizen, she's also highly reasonable, so she'd never complain about non-participation in a holiday that wasn't hers to begin with; and (3) we were all happy to have me go with her and snag all the turkey I could eat.

"Holidays aren't my thing," The Man said now with a shrug.

You know, maybe he could've gotten away with it. If he hadn't said the not "my thing" part or if he'd left off the casual shrug, maybe he could've skated this time. But the nonchalant combo of the two?

"*Holidays* don't have to be your *thing*," New Woman said. "So what if it's not your *thing*? What is this insistence everyone has these days on only doing things if those things are a person's *thing*?"

"I just meant that I'm not really comfortable with—"

"And whoever said anything about needing to be *comfortable* all the time? For *comfortable*, you have those flannel shirts, which you wear every day."

"Hey, that's not fair! You wear them too!"

"I don't know where anyone ever gave you the idea that holidays were supposed to be *comfortable*. Holidays are about *family*."

"Well, it's not very important to—"

Aaaaaand that's when I started barking my fool head off. Hey, someone had to stop him before that next irrevocable word came out of his mouth.

But as soon as I stopped barking, he opened his mouth to speak some more, so I started barking like crazy again.

"Gatz, what is it?" he said at last.

After his therapy session, he'd had the revelation that he said no too often, that maybe if he said yes to stuff sometimes, it'd be like saying yes to life, yes to love, and then who knows? Maybe a little yes now would keep this relationship alive where his previous one had failed.

Of course he picked up what I was putting down. He sat up in bed. "Yeah, um, this whole Thanksgiving thing," The Man said. "What exactly did you have in mind?"

Chapter Seventeen

Thanksgiving

A lot of holidays come equipped with an eve component, and Thanksgiving proved no different. Normally, I spend holidays with The Woman, but when she learned that The Man was going to be actually spending the day with families—plural!—she took pity on him. And just like how he'd insisted she keep me during the weekdays when she'd been sending out her résumé, she insisted he keep me now.

"I can't believe you're going to your family for a holiday," she said when he'd stopped by her place to drop me off.

"Yeah, well . . ."

"And her family too?"

"Yeah, well . . ."

"You must really like her," she observed. "She must've become very important for you to subject yourself to *two* families on the same day."

Here, The Man let a genuine smile play across his face as he nodded agreement.

A lesser person, a less mature person, might've made a jab at this point, something along the lines of "When we were together, you wouldn't do that for me." The Woman, though, has never been lesser.

"You'll really need Gatz, then," she said, "to help you get through the day. Gatz is the perfect icebreaker."

"But what about you?" The Man said. "You always said how much your family loves seeing Gatz, especially your nieces and nephews."

"They do, but I'm not going there this year."

"You're not going to your family for Thanksgiving?"

"Nope," she said.

"You're going to spend it with his family?"

"They live in Indiana, and, nope, we're not going there either."

The Woman not spending a holiday with any family, hers or New Man's, was as surprising a development as the fact that The Man was.

"I don't get it," The Man said.

"I'm just not feeling it this year," she said. "I think I just need some time to regroup, so we'll spend a quiet day here, just the two of us. Really, you take Gatz. I'll be fine."

I gotta admit to being a bit worried about her then, but one thing I did agree was fine: the great generosity of spirit they were showing toward each other, the way each was willing to give up their usual time with me if they thought the other needed me more.

Thanksgiving Day itself dawned with me waking to the smell of baking. I figured it must be coming from some other apartment in the building, or maybe even outside, but as I sniffed the air and registered the strength of the smells, I realized it was coming from: *inside our place*.

Someone was baking?

Not a usual event around here, so I leaped from the couch and padded toward the kitchen to investigate, while at the same time The Man emerged from the bedroom in a bathrobe, scratching his head and padding toward the kitchen too, also apparently curious.

We both found New Woman in there, hard at work. I figured

she'd popped in early or had even decided to spend the night after I fell asleep. She did that now sometimes. I guess you could leave a cat like Hoops alone overnight: Hoops didn't need to be taken out for walks and could be depended upon to make however much food was in the bowl last until his owner came through the door again. Such an arrangement would never work for me.

"What are you making?" The Man asked.

"I'm making crustless cranberry pies. It's a bit nontraditional, and I love making pumpkin pies, but I don't want to make anything that directly competes with what the hostess is no doubt making."

"You call your mom 'the hostess'?"

"Of course not. That would be your mom. I'm making two: one for my family and one for yours."

"But I told you we don't need to bring anything."

"That's ridiculous. I asked you to ask your mom what I could bring. If you'd done that, I wouldn't have to guess at what she might like."

"Look, I know her. She doesn't like people to bring stuff. She won't be happy about it."

"More ridiculousness. I'm not going to meet your parents for the first time empty-handed. I wasn't raised by wolves."

For the first time, it occurred to The Man to wonder: "Should I have bought something to bring to your parents' place later?"

"Nah, I've got you covered. If you can find some tinfoil in this place and help me cover them, I'll say we made the pie together."

Finding some tinfoil in our place proved more challenging than one might imagine, but eventually success was achieved, The Man showered for the first time in a few days and got dressed in his usual, only cleaner, while New Woman put on a dress for the first time since I'd met her, leaving the ball cap behind. When he saw what she was wearing, and after I barked my opinion at him, he quickly swapped his flannel for a nicer button-down. Finally, we were ready to dust off The Man's car and hit the road, first to The Man's family in Westchester.

As I bounced along in the back seat next to the covered pies, I wasn't tempted to steal a bite. I'm not really much of a cranberry guy.

But I was tempted by the prospect of meeting The Man's parents, whom I'd only ever heard stories about.

Chapter Eighteen

Still Thanksgiving . . .

It's not like there hadn't been . . . *inklings* that The Man's parents . . . *might not be the best.*

There was the fact that the only time he and The Woman had gone there, for a Hanukkah celebration, he'd come home upset.

There was the fact that even though he still did see them sometimes, it was always at their place, he always went by himself, and he always returned home upset.

And there was the fact that I'd never met them, not even once.

Still, as we pulled up in front of a house that was relatively modest for the street it was on, I found myself wondering what I'd often wondered: How bad could they really be, if they raised The Man, whom I loved so much?

"Who's your little, uh, *friend*?" The Man's Mother said after opening the door, raising an over-tweezed eyebrow at him and then me. She had a wool suit on and pearls, portrait of an old-school matron in a town full of Lululemon matrons.

"It's Gatz. Remember? I called yesterday and said I'd be bringing him too."

"Of course. Did you bring your own chain?"

"My own *chain*?"

"You know, so we can tie him up outside."

"He's not a dog that needs to be chained up, Mother. Gatz is very well behaved. He'll be fine inside, with us."

"Well, if you're sure . . ." she said, standing aside finally with the greatest reluctance and opening the door just wide enough to let us in.

"And who's this?" The Man's Mother said, looking at New Woman.

"I told you I'd be bringing a guest," he said.

"You did," she allowed. "But you never mentioned that she'd be so . . ."

And then she simply let that "so" hang in the air, leaving us all to wonder what would have followed and to fill in the blanks for ourselves. I kind of hoped she meant "pretty," but I had my doubts.

"Thank you for inviting me," New Woman said, juggling the pie she was holding from her right side to her left and putting her hand out for a shake. The Man's Mother didn't offer hers back, so New Woman just stretched her hand farther, took one of the hands The Man's Mother had hanging limply by her sides, and gave it a warm jiggle. "Here, I made this for you." She offered up the pie.

"What's this?" The Man's Mother said.

"It's pie. Just a little cranberry thing I whipped together."

"Oh. But I already have pumpkin. I'll just put this . . ." She turned to The Man. "Please go get your father. Tell him it's time for dinner."

At least she said "please." But wait. No cocktail hour? No hors d'oeuvres? Just straight to the table?

New Woman and I went with The Man to a living room–like space, unlike any I'd seen before, with thick plastic covering all the furniture, the plastic making squeaking noises as The Man's Father uncrossed and recrossed his legs, head buried in the newspaper.

"Um, Dad?" The Man said.

"Oh, hello!" The Man's Father said, dropping his paper enough to see us. "You're here!"

"Yes," The Man said, "and this is Gatz and this is—"

"Lovely, just lovely, I'm sure!" The Man's Father said, discarding the paper entirely. "Well." He rose to his feet. "Must be time for me to carve the turkey!"

It wasn't until he was walking away that it occurred to me that neither the mother nor the father had hugged The Man hello. They hadn't touched him at all.

"They're just a little . . ." The Man said quietly, embarrassed.

"It's OK," New Woman said. "Really, it's OK."

"I did try to warn you."

"And I believed you. But it's going to be fine."

I couldn't see how she could be so sure of that. To offer moral support, I rubbed my head against The Man's lower leg.

"Thanks, Gatz," he said.

While I knew we were having a heartfelt moment, it did occur to me that it had been too long since I'd had my last meal and this was supposed to be a holiday and holidays were known for their belly-busting quantities of food . . .

I broke from the group and tore off in what was the logical direction for the dining room to be.

"No, Gatz!" The Man yelled.

Immediately, I stopped in my tracks, right in front of the dining room table.

Just as immediately, The Man's Mother poked her head out from the kitchen. "I thought you said he could behave himself?"

"He can."

She skeptically looked down at me, a darkness behind her eyes. Sheesh.

"How can I help?" New Woman offered, following her into the kitchen.

"We've got everything under control," The Man's Mother said.

"Totally under control!" The Man's Father said.

"Don't be ridiculous," New Woman said.

And New Woman proceeded to go back and forth, bringing platters from one room to the other, not that there were very many platters to bring. She'd bring one out and set it down, The Man's Mother would come out and move it somewhere else, and so on like that.

All the while, The Man crouched next to me, arms draped loosely around my neck. At first I thought he was doing it to restrain me; you know, so I wouldn't run at the table again. But honestly, it's not like there were any great odors in the air, like you'd expect, so I wasn't overcome any more with impulses to run at the table. And after a while, I figured he just needed a hug.

"OK, we're all set," The Man's Mother said.

"Great," The Man said. "First, let me just . . ."

Then he led me to the kitchen, where he got out a little plate and put some incredibly dry-looking turkey slices on it for me, and set it on the kitchen floor.

I was used to my holidays with The Woman's family, where everyone made a fuss over me (in a good way), where I was welcome near the dining room table (if not necessarily on the table), where there was an overabundance of amazing food, and where I was served whatever I wanted on a fine china plate.

"I'm sorry," The Man whispered apologetically. "We won't be here very long." He lowered his voice still further to add, "I'd have given you some of the mashed potatoes too, but trust me on this, you wouldn't like it."

Then, with a sigh, he rose to his feet and went to join the others, leaving me to listen in on the conversation as I picked at my dry turkey, which was actively bad. I ate it all, but I didn't like it. It occurred to me then that the whole house didn't smell the way Thanksgiving was supposed to either. It smelled like . . . nothing.

Not being able to observe the others, all I could do was take in the dialogue.

The Man's Mother: "Are you still writing?"

The Man: "Of course I'm still writing. Do you ask other people, like accountants or doctors, 'Are you still accounting and doctoring?' Writing isn't a temporary whim."

The Man's Mother: "It was a legitimate question."

The Man's Father: "Are you making any money at it?"

The Man: "Have I ever asked you for any money?"

The Man's Father: "No."

The Man: "Well then, unless I'm secretly robbing banks on the side, I must be making money."

The Man's Father: "But it's not great money. I hear the only way you can make great money as a writer is if you're one of those bestsellers. Are you one of those bestsellers yet?"

I imagined he knew the answer to that question already.

The Man: "No, not yet, but I'll keep that in mind."

The Man's Father let out a long sigh.

The Man: "What?"

The Man's Father: "Oh, nothing, nothing."

The sound of forks clinking on china resumed; the vibration of voices lulled.

It occurred to me then that New Woman was uncharacteristically silent.

It made me wonder if she was feeling the things I was feeling, almost tempted to laugh at how ridiculously awful they were while at the same time heartbroken to think he'd grown up with these people who had no warmth and clearly no belief in him. It explained a lot about the voices inside that drove him and tormented him, and the darkness that sometimes became too dark for him to fend off.

In a way, I was surprised to hear that, if only with sarcasm, he was at least defending himself.

The Man's Mother: "And how about you? What do you do?"

New Woman: "I'm a writer."

The Man's Mother: "Oh, and—"

New Woman: "I'm the same kind of writer your son is."

The Man's Father: "And what—"

New Woman: "I write fiction books that aren't great-money bestsellers, so I doubt you'd be proud to have your friends read them, but I make enough money to support myself. And while we're on the subject, do you have any idea what an amazing writer your son is? Every sentence counts; every word counts. That might not mean anything to you, but trust me, it means a lot to the *New York Times*. And *Kirkus*! Don't get me started on *Kirkus*! OK, fine, I'll get started on *Kirkus*. Let's just say that every single book he's written has received a starred review from them. Every. Single. One. Stars! From *Kirkus*! Now go ahead and try to tell me what other writers have accomplished this, while I just sit here and wait. On second thought, that should take you a while, so I'll clear the table."

I poked my head around the corner to get a glimpse at the scene. As she carried plates to the kitchen, The Man watched her go with admiration. I'd never heard anyone speak up for him like that before. The Man's Mother and The Man's Father sat there in silent shock. New Woman returned to the dining room and dropped the pumpkin pie down in the middle of the table with a light thud. I ducked back behind the kitchen island.

Pie was served in silence, pie was consumed in silence, and before we knew it, we were back at the door again, saying our goodbyes.

"Just as I suspected," The Man's Mother said, "with my pumpkin pie, we didn't need any other desserts. We appreciate it, though." She handed the cranberry pie back to New Woman.

"When do you want us for Hanukkah?" New Woman asked.

"Excuse me?"

"Hanukkah. You know. Eight nights of latkes? Festival of Lights? I know it falls on different dates every year, and I haven't mastered the lunar calendar yet, so you'll have to let us know what night will work best. Well." Then before she could be stopped, she planted a kiss on The Man's Mother's cheek and headed for the car, throwing a waving hand behind her. "Thanks again!"

The Man kept his eyes forward, looking through his mother instead of at her. She looked down at me again, and when I met her glance, she almost looked curious. To her son: "Do me a favor?"

He met her eye.

"Look after yourself. She's not . . . she's not the right kind of person for you."

The door shut in his face.

"You want to go back *there* for Hanukkah," The Man deadpanned once we were all back in the car.

"No, of course not. But we're going. You'll make sure she invites us and we'll go when she does."

"I'm sorry you had to go through that. But they're awful. They're every bit as awful as I told you they were."

"Worse, even! But they're your family. We're going."

The Man shook his head as he keyed up the ignition. Then he turned to look over his right shoulder so he could see through the back window to reverse.

That's when New Woman smacked a big wet one on his cheek. *MWAH!*

"I love you," she said. "You're you in spite of those loons, not because of them."

He smiled down at her and she turned to me, rubbing me behind the ears from her seat. But I still caught the moment when The Man looked through the front windshield after reversing and noticed his mother standing at the living room curtain, peeking out at her son around the edge. At their eye contact, she dropped the curtain and disappeared from sight.

Chapter Nineteen

Still Thanksgiving!

If The Man's family lived in the smallest house on a big-house block, then New Woman's family lived in the biggest house on a small-house block; I saw as we pulled up in front of the corner Victorian about an hour later.

If I'd just had reinforced for me why The Man was not big on family because his was the opposite of wonderful, it would've been safe to assume that the reason New Woman was big on family was because hers was simply amazing, right?

Well, heh. Heh-heh-heh-heh-heh.

"They're here, they're here, they're heeeeeere!" a short and rather round woman shouted, charging out the screen door and letting it slam behind her. She waddled down the walk, throwing her arms around New Woman. "Oh, I thought you'd never come! But look at you." She stood back. "Is that a dress? I can't believe my eyes."

"Well, Mami," New Woman said, "first we went to—"

"Oh, of course, I remember now. The *other* parents. So long as you're putting on a dress for someone, I won't complain. And you must be—" She reached up, enveloping The Man in a tight hug that almost knocked him off his feet. "And Gatz!" Now it was my turn, and while it beat the chilliness of The Man's Mother, it was, well, a lot.

"Come in, come in! Everyone's been waiting!"

Upon entering, we were enthusiastically introduced around and I learned who "everyone" entailed, which turned out to be mostly a ton of uncles and aunts, cousins, and their kids. But like The Man, New Woman had no siblings.

"Oh, believe me," Mami said, "I wanted to fill this house with kids—that's why we bought such a big place!" Neither The Man nor I had asked anything to solicit this confession.

It occurred to me then what I had on my hands here: an over-sharer.

"Believe me, we tried," Mami said, "but the Lord had other plans for me."

There was still one person we hadn't been introduced to, a big silent guy in the corner.

"Papi!" New Woman cried, going over to hug him.

He grunted, but the all-over-his-face smile told me everything I needed to know about him. He was thrilled his little girl was so happy to see him.

Before he could say anything, though, Mami was back with, "Ooh, what's that you brought?"

"It's just a little cranberry—"

"Oh, it looks so wonderful! Did everyone see? I need to find a very special plate for it!"

"Really, it's just—"

But I was quickly learning, there was no stopping Mami on a mission. And I was also quickly learning that it didn't really matter how many people were in the room, and there were a lot. Because if Mami was there, there really wasn't room for anybody else.

"OK, now that's in the center of the table, right where it belongs, it's so beautiful. Now, everyone gather round, we need to say grace first. Now that's done, everybody start passing the plates around, everyone go clockwise. You! Why did you just go counterclockwise? Did you not hear me say . . . And oh my goodness gracious, what about Gatz? Where are my manners?"

She went to the kitchen, returned with a plate for me, started to put some turkey on it, stopped and looked at The Man. "I didn't even think to ask. Does Gatz prefer light meat? Dark meat? A wing? A leg?"

"Gatz loves, um, any kind of meat. So long as it's, um, yeah, meat."

"Maybe you should do it, then? Oh, of course you shouldn't do it, you're our guest—although, already, you feel like family! But I can do it. I'll give Gatz a little bit of each and . . ."

By the time she delivered the plate to me on the floor, it was heaped so high, I wasn't sure where to start. And it smelled really, really good too. But it was overwhelming, and when Papi eyed the giant breast she'd given me, I thought maybe she'd gone too far.

"Don't you let him guilt you into giving that turkey up, Gatz," she told me. "You eat as much as you want and let me know when you want more."

Next Tuesday, maybe?

"Now, then," Mami said. And she turned her attention fully to New Woman.

And the questions started. And the comments.

"Do you eat enough? Because I don't think you look like you eat enough. And how is the writing going? I loved those pages you sent me, but I had some ideas. And that cover for your last book was pretty. But maybe your publisher should make the next one more pretty? You know, I see those books that get picked up by those big book clubs and they all seem to share a certain . . . *something*. Do you know what I'm talking about? That something? And I just think that your books, because they're better than all the other books out there, deserve to have that something, whatever it is, so the whole world will know what I know, which is that you are simply the best there is."

I won't claim Mami said all that in one go, because such was not the case. Whenever Mami would pause for a bite of food or a sip of wine or to take a breath, New Woman would demur or explain whatever was the appropriate response to whatever Mami had said, as in "I'm not the best there is, and that's not false modesty, it's that 'best' is entirely subjective" or "Writers at my level may get invited to suggest what we hope to see on the cover, but it's ultimately the publisher and their art department who get the final say . . ."

Like that.

But Mami wasn't having it and would always counter with "Of course you're the best; I should know because who's more objective about you than me?" and "I bet all you need to do is assert yourself a bit more, tell the publisher how you want it to be, and I'm sure they'll listen."

If The Man's problem was that he had been loved too little growing up, that his parents were too cold, then New Woman's problem was that she had been loved too much. Mami was wonderful in her own way, don't get me wrong. I mean, what's not to love about being fed like a king? But Mami had her own faults too, because Mami was a smotherer, and she didn't seem to hear her daughter at all.

It can't have been easy for New Woman growing up like that, constantly listening to someone else insist that your shit does not and could never stink, when your own evidence to the contrary tells you that, yes, occasionally, it does.

The thing was, you could see that New Woman was used to it, she bore it with as much grace and dignity and patience as anyone could, but being the sole focus of all that laser-like attention: it was a lot.

And then Mami turned her attention to The Man.

"I'm so glad you could come and that she brought you and Gatz. You know, she told me you're a writer too, and I'm sure you're also very good, I bet you're the second-best writer on the planet, but tell me, because I'm just curious: Are you Catholic?"

Chapter Twenty

Even Thanksgiving has a tail . . .

OK, so who had "Mami will say that Jewish could be *almost* as good as Catholic but *only* if it's *practicing*" on their Thanksgiving bingo card?

Yeah, me neither.

"Do you know how crazy that sounds to me?" The Man said as we drove our way back to the city afterward.

Well, who could blame him? It sounded pretty crazy to me too.

"But don't you get it?" New Woman said. "That's the way she thinks."

"I thought I was going to fall off my chair when she said, 'At least you're not Protestant.' Was she trying to make me feel better?"

"Never. If she says it, it's because she absolutely believes it."

"But when I told her I was nonpracticing . . ."

". . . she almost fell off *her* chair." New Woman sighed. "Look, I'd never ask you to convert . . ."

"Thank you."

"And she wouldn't ask you to either. Mami wouldn't want you to fake believe."

"Good, because I don't think I could do that."

"But if someday we were ever to get married—and I'm not saying that that's something we'll ever do!—I know she'd be more comfortable if you practiced a religion. It's like she'd respect the union more if you were some kind of religious. But not Protestant."

"So, I'd what? Need to become more Jewish to please your Catholic mom?"

"She is how she is."

"Crazy." The Man shook his head. But then, in the darkness of the car, I could see him smile as he took her hand.

I knew before this was all over, I'd wind up in a yarmulke.

And I also knew, when we got home, that The Man had done good. And I knew this because:

"You done good," New Woman said, removing his Mets cap and flinging it onto the sofa, landing another big wet one on him, smack on the lips. Then she reached over her shoulders and began slowly pulling down her dress zipper.

"So there are benefits to having done good," The Man said, kissing her neck, helping her with the zipper.

"Most definitely."

"You know, in a sense, your family situation is just as bad as mine."

"Worse! At least you can get some space. Me, if I don't go, I feel guilty. And if I go, I'm smothered."

"But we'll still go see them?"

"On Hanukkah and Christmas."

"Because family?"

"Because family."

Well, they understood what they meant.

And they also understood what they meant when The Man retrieved his Mets cap from the couch, gently slapped it on her head, and said, "Now I'm really in the mood." She laughed, they kissed deeply, hand in hand they ran off to the bedroom, and soon thereafter I heard the mattress shaking.

Me, I was just happy that we'd all survived the day and had returned home bearing lots of leftovers.

Chapter Twenty-One

Some day in November . . .

It was getting to the point where I didn't even always know what day it was anymore. Before, I always knew I had five nights with The Man and two nights with The Woman, all very easy to keep track of.

But when The Man dropped me off at The Woman's that morning, I was all in a mental quandary. *Is it Friday? Is it Saturday?*

"Was Gatz helpful?" The Woman asked.

"Gatz is always helpful," The Man said. "But yes, on this particular occasion, I'm not sure how I would've gotten through it all without him. Oh, hey, I brought you this."

He handed over a double bag he'd been carrying.

The Woman held it to her face and closed her eyes as she inhaled. "Mmm, this smells heavenly," she said. Opening her eyes, she frowned. "This isn't your mother's cooking, is it? Because I do remember that one time we went—"

"Oh, no." The Man laughed. "Gosh, no. We—well, she—made it at my place."

"Right," The Woman said. "Well, it seems like you all had a good day. I'm glad."

"Thanks." Awkward shuffling of feet. "So, what are your plans for Black Friday?"

Thank you! Of course. Yesterday was Thanksgiving, always a Thursday, so today was naturally

"Nothing," she said with a shrug.

Nothing? But she always went shopping with her mom on Black Friday! She loved doing that, or at least loved having the day off from work because of the long holiday weekend. Of course, this year we hadn't gone to her parents' place in the Hamptons, so there'd be no shopping for her and her mom today, no fashion show for Gatz when they returned home with all their purchases.

I slumped down onto the ground, letting my fur taketh me over.

She forced a smile around sad eyes. "And you? How are you going to spend the day? Writing?"

More awkward arm swinging. "Shopping."

She looked skeptical. "But you *hate* shopping . . ."

"Shopping for a synagogue."

She burst out laughing until she quickly simmered down upon seeing the expression on his face. "Oh! Oh, you're serious."

"Yup!" He nodded, smiling goofily.

Man, I loved that goofy smile.

"Life's really growing bigger for you, isn't it?"

He started to nod, but he knew that look of sorrow.

"Hey . . ." He reached out a hand, awkwardly rubbing her upper arm. "It'll be okay."

She gave him a quick peck on the cheek, then pushed him so he was facing the other way and propelled him toward the door.

"Out of here, you," she said. "I'm fine. Really. Now, you get on with your synagogue shopping."

She even sounded pretty chipper when she said all that, but once he was gone, she stood with her back against the door, looking deflated.

"Now what do we do, Gatz?"

We could eat some leftovers.

"You're probably hungry."

I could eat.

We went to the kitchen, and while she prepared a couple of plates for us, I looked around, puzzled. Where was New Man?

"He's started working on a new book," she said, giving a chin-nod toward his office. "I doubt he'd notice if a bomb got set off in here."

Now, that wasn't really fair. Yes, I always had The Woman's back. It was practically in my job description. But . . .

Come on! The guy's a writer! Having to write when the muse hits him is practically in his description. As a former editor—who I know will be hired very soon!—you know this.

But that was part of the problem, wasn't it? How much of him had I seen lately?

"I know," she said with a sigh. "It isn't really his fault. Maybe it's my fault."

Your fault? Nothing is ever your fault. You're The Woman!

"That's what I get for getting involved with back-to-back writers." And another sigh.

The sighing was bad enough, from one who wasn't by natural disposition a sigher, but the actual words she was speaking? It made it sound like she was having second thoughts about New Man. But she couldn't be having second thoughts about New Man. He was The One! And he wasn't just any writer. He was her fiancé!

Just then, New Man emerged from where he'd been working, swept her up in his arms, and laid a big kiss on her.

Releasing her, he said with a rakish grin, "Sorry, I just needed some inspiration." Another grin. "Gotta get back to it now."

And he was off again.

In a way, it was romantic, that he needed an infusion of her to keep going. But it was also so hit-and-run, which is exactly how she looked: stunned.

My inclination was to jump to his defense on this—as a writer, he couldn't be blamed for not noticing if a bomb went off in here, not while he was deep in work. But one thing a committed fiancé should've noticed was . . .

Doesn't he see you're looking kind of depressed?

Because as I had a chance to study her better, now that we were alone together, she didn't look right. She'd always been so stylish. Even when at home and wearing her comfies, they were still always stylish comfies. But as I eyed her from hair that looked like it was overdue for a rebraiding to feet clad in thick socks rolled around the ankles at disparate lengths, it occurred to me: it's one thing to be *hygge* after work, as a respite from the daily grind, but no one should be doing *hygge* twenty-four seven.

Come to think of it, they hadn't even been shaking the mattress as much as they used to lately.

So as we ate our plates of leftover turkey and spuds together, I began plotting in my brain:

How can I convince her to do something resembling a fun Black Friday activity today?

Chapter Twenty-Two

Black Friday afternoon . . .

Rarely do I find myself lamenting my inability to speak words aloud. Yes, The Man makes his living with the written word, and I have the highest respect for that. But while humans like to go on and on about how it's not what people say, it's their actions that speak louder, it seems to me that throughout the history of humankind, it's a lot of their talk-talk-talking that gets humans into so much trouble. But then there are those occasions when that ability sure would come in handy . . .

I cast my eyes about the penthouse, sniffing here and there, trying to come up with a way to convey to The Woman just what exactly I had in mind to snap her out of it. I confess to briefly getting distracted by a chew toy while nosing through my toy basket for inspiration, but eventually I was able to tear myself away from all that tempting chewy rubber. And eventually, I found what I was looking for in New Man's office.

"Oh, hey, Gatz!" New Man said, looking up briefly from his laptop. "When did you get in?"

There, I thought with satisfaction. He may not notice a bomb, but he still notices the Gatzer. *So he's not too far gone, in the oblivion department, for a writer.*

I trotted over to him, bowed my head, and let him scratch me behind the ears for a while, because it would be rude not to acknowledge his greeting. But all the while I was thinking:

Not you. You're not the inspiration I was looking for.

At last, when he'd had his fill of the supremely enjoyable activity of scratching me and the half-filled page in his open document commanded the return of his attention, I was able to resume my mission.

I found just what I needed right there on the table:

The stack of magazines.

Every now and then, you hear people proclaiming: "Print is dead!"

Well, not if The Woman could help it. No one believed in the printed word more. Except maybe The Man, New Man, and New Woman. And all the other writers, editors, and publishing types in the world. And a ton of the people who call themselves readers.

Yeah, screw "Print is dead!"

Anyway, the magazine on top wasn't the one I was looking for, so I pushed it with my nose until it fell off the top of the stack and onto the table, making a mild *thud* sound.

"Did you need help with something, Gatz?"

Nope, got it.

I proceeded to knock magazines off, one at a time, knocking almost all of them off and creating quite a mess on the table and floor, until only one was left.

There it was.

I knocked that one to the floor too, leaped down after it, and, grabbing a few pages between my teeth, began dragging it from the room.

"You sure you don't need some help with that, Gatz?"

Nope, everything's under control.

I dragged it all the way out to the other room, where I found The Woman staring out the window, and dropped it at her feet. My teeth had left a lot of marks, which I saw on the back cover after I dropped it, but the whole was pretty much intact.

"Fetch?" she said, shrugging. She picked up the magazine, tore off the back cover, began to crumple it.

No, not—

She got into a half-hearted pitcher's pose with the crumpled-up page and tossed it. But it didn't go very far. Still, despite the lack of a real challenge, it took everything in me not to follow my instincts and chase it down.

She looked at me still standing there and looked at the abandoned crumpled paper. She looked so defeated then, curled up and small against the window.

I nudged the magazine with my snout until I managed to flip it over. The cover revealed a grinning bride in a long white gown. The Woman gazed down at it somberly.

I nudged it closer to her.

"What are you trying to tell me, Gatz?"

Using snout and paws, I managed to flip some pages, even if I created rips in almost all the pages I flipped, hoping she was seeing what I was seeing, like: *Look at all the pretty dresses!*

"I don't feel like going out to shop right now—"

I looked around, found her laptop, gave it a nudge.

"I suppose I could shop online, but who wants to shop for a wedding dress alone?" She cast her eyes in the direction of his office. "I suppose I could ask him, but I don't want to interrupt his work."

You can't afford to wait. You need something to occupy your mind right now!

"Plus, it'd be bad luck to have the groom see the dress before the wedding, even if only in a picture."

Exactly.

"But I still don't want—"

I trotted halfway to the kitchen, glanced over my shoulder, and gave her my best come-hither look, compelling her to follow me, which she did.

Once there, I hopped up on the counter and nudged her cell phone toward her.

"Phone a friend? But it's a holiday weekend. No one will be free on such short notice."

I nudged the phone closer.

Call them! They're you're friends! You're there for everyone else when they need you. They should be there for you! What kind of friends would they be if they're not?

With a sigh, The Woman picked up her phone rather listlessly, like she expected nothing good would come of it, but at least she began calling around.

Turned out, ol' Gatz was right.

Turned out, if her BFFs weren't free, they'd make themselves free. And before we knew it, The Blonde, The Redhead, and The Brunette all came bustling in, dispensing enthusiastic kisses and hugs and bearing bottles. Only this time, instead of the usual wine, everyone brought champagne.

What a great idea for a celebration!

It took a while for the smile on The Woman's lips to get all the way to her eyes, but it made it. Day-drinking can have that effect, plus the support of great friends.

A lot of hilarity ensued as they gathered around the laptop, going through pages and pages of dresses, some of them quite pretty, some of them hellacious.

At one point, right when they were looking at a particularly gorgeous gown, a real contender, New Man came through on his way to the kitchen.

"Hey, what are you all—" he started to say.

Immediately, The Woman pulled the top of the laptop closed while her friends gathered closer in an overcautious attempt to shield from view that which was no longer in view.

"You can't look!" they all cried, quite schoolgirlish and very charming. And a little drunk.

He raised his hands in a no-problem gesture, backing away.

The Woman broke from the group, ran over, and threw her arms around his neck. Now it was her turn to hit-and-run him in the kiss department. When they finally broke for air, he looked stunned but also incredibly pleased.

"I just love you," she said.

See? Her spirits were doing better already.

After he got whatever he needed from the kitchen and went back to work, she returned to the group.

While they were looking at more bridal dresses, she said, "And of course I'll want you to help pick your own dresses. I wouldn't want you to wear anything you'd hate."

"We're your bridesmaids?" The Brunette squealed, clasped hands to heart.

"I can't imagine asking anyone else," The Woman said.

"Who are his groomsmen going to be?" The Redhead asked.

"My brothers," The Woman said. Then she named two other guys.

"They're huge bestsellers!" The Blonde said, her eyes going wide.

Huger than New Man? Guess those guys all stick together.

"Like, mega," The Brunette added. "They're *mega* bestsellers!"

"Maybe we can poach them," The Blonde suggested.

"I don't think that's really the point of this," mentioned The Redhead.

"But if he's got four," The Brunette said, "don't you need a fourth too?"

"I figured I'll ask his sister," she said.

"But you haven't?" The Redhead pressed.

"I haven't met her yet," The Woman said. "For a long time, I was busy with work. And lately I've been busy with . . . whatever I've been busy with. But when we drive out to Indiana for Christmas, I'll do it then. I want to do it in person."

"Indiana?" The Brunette said. "Why would you drive all the way to Indiana?"

"He hates flying," The Woman said. "He only does it when he absolutely has to, but the whole thing terrifies him, so he'd rather drive. And why not? Since now I've got nothing but time . . ."

No one said anything about that, and a moment of silence was shared by all in honor of her former career.

"Let's look at more dresses!" The Woman said brightly, breaking the silence. "And have more champagne!" A few minutes later, she added, "You know, I bet I could do all my planning on here: find a venue, pick out flowers, you name it."

She seemed enthusiastic and I knew that, with her organizational skills, she'd throw herself into it and become the best self–wedding planner in history.

See? The ol' Gatzer was right. All she needed was a new hobby.

Chapter Twenty-Three

December

The Editor had come for a visit, bringing up the topic of media training for The Man again, but this time, he was even more serious about it. Hearing that, The Man had retched, putting one hand over his mouth and running for the bathroom. And seeing *that*, The Editor discreetly departed.

Now, New Woman had stopped by, at The Man's request, to talk him off his ledge.

I don't know what I was expecting . . . that New Woman would handle it the way The Woman would have, with a lot of soothing words accompanied by a supremely serene presence? Had I not *met* New Woman? Because instead of balm and calm, she came up with:

"What the hell is the *matter* with you?"

She'd stormed right through the front door. Me and The Man? We were sacked out on the couch, which I'd been trying to pull him off with my teeth all day.

Finally, a little help around here.

He sighed and sat up, burying his tired face in his hands. "I thought you, of all people, would understand."

"Every author at our level would *kill* for an opportunity like this; *I* would kill for an opportunity like this. To be sent out on a real tour like the big guys get?"

"You mean you wouldn't mind it?"

"Are you kidding me? I would ha-ha-ha-*hate* it, every single miserable second. I would want to tear my hair out; I would want to scream; I would rue the day I ever got the calling to be a writer and would vow to curse Jo March until the day I died."

"So you understand. You'd say no too?"

"I'd want to, but I wouldn't. Despite how bad it's going to be, it's too good to pass up. So I'd say yes, which is what you're going to do too."

"Aw, *man*! But I don't even really understand what media training is; I'm not a media training guy, I'd be so bad doing that. Do you know what it is?"

"Of course not. But you'll learn. Then you can teach me, in case I'm ever lucky enough to need it."

"Aw, *man*." The Man groaned, knowing she was right.

"It's not like anything's going to happen right away, anyway," New Woman said. "Your book's not coming out for almost a year. So think about how lucky you are! Not only does your publisher really want to get behind you on this one, but your editor knows you so well, he knows to give you plenty of time to wrap your head around it and prepare."

I watched The Man digest her input, and I lolled my tongue to show my approval. But my lolling lulled to a stop when I saw how defeated this suggestion made The Man feel. She got up to make a snack and he leaned back into the couch replying one last time, but with far less conviction: "Aw, man."

Chapter Twenty-Four

Not on land . . .

We were going sailing . . . in December!

OK, we weren't actually going to take the boat out of its dock, but the forecast for that weekend was for one of those climate-change December days where the temperature was to soar over seventy and skies were expected to be clear.

One of New Man's two mega-bestselling author friends, the guys who were going to be his groomsmen, apparently had a really big boat. Let's just call him Mega Bestseller #1. They were dying to meet The Woman—who wouldn't be!—and New Man was dying for them to meet her, which was totally understandable, since she was quite the catch. So a plan had been hatched for everyone to go sailing, but not sailing. They'd eat the best food and drink the best beverages, all while experiencing the sun on their faces and the wind in their hair. What could be better?

Mega Bestseller #2 even planned to charter a helicopter to avoid traffic and get everyone out there quicker. When I heard that, I grew even more excited. I loved the idea of going up in a whirlybird! I was sure it would be like riding in a convertible car only on steroids because we'd be in the sky.

But that was not to be.

"You know I hate—" New Man started to say.

"Flying," The Woman finished for him.

"It's the only thing that ever scares me. That, and dogs that aren't Gatz."

Well, who wouldn't be charmed by that?

"So, I guess we'll just drive a really long time to get there instead?" The Woman said.

So that's what we did. And it really wasn't too much of a letdown, because New Man does own a convertible, so I still got to have the whole wind-in-my-fur experience, and the tunes were good.

But it sure took a long time to get there that way.

By the time we did get there, found a place to park, and located the right mooring, from the shouts and laughter coming from the vessel, it sounded like the party had been going on quite some time without us.

And the size of the boat! I'm not accusing anyone of overcompensating here, but why would a single male need something of that . . . *size*?

As we approached, I looked up to see four people lining the railing of the upper deck, two men and two bikini-clad women. They all had long drinks with umbrellas sticking out of them, and both of the men had their arms around the women.

"Ahoy!" one of the men yelled, raising his glass aloft. He did it in a proprietary I'm-in-charge kind of way, leading me to believe he must be Mega Bestseller #1, owner of the boat.

"Ahoy!" New Man yelled back as we stepped onto the gangway. "Permission to come aboard?"

I found his question to be a bit dorky, but New Man is so nearly perfect and makes so few faux pas, I was inclined to let this one pass.

"Permission granted!" Mega Bestseller #1 shouted. OK, now, that really was too dorky for words; entitled, too. How come no one told me I was going to be spending the day with entitled people?

And how come no one told me how slippery a highly polished teak deck was going to be beneath my paws? Damn! It was so exciting!

I'd run onto the deck ahead of the others, sliding across it and turning in time to hear Mega Bestseller #2 say, "Here, allow me," as he reached a palm out and elegantly handed The Woman onto the deck.

There were handshakes and air-kisses all around as introductions were made.

As always, there was a lot of exclaiming over me.

"Gatz!" Bikini #1 said. "What a great name!"

"How'd you come up with that?" Bikini #2 said.

"From Gatsby," The Woman said.

Blank stares.

"As in *The Great Gatsby*?" she tried again.

More blank stares.

Wow, that had never happened to me before, people not immediately getting the literary connection, once it was explained to them, to arguably the greatest literary novel ever. For all these two knew, Gatz might just as well be some garden-variety doggy name, like Spot or Rover or, heaven forbid, Fido.

"It doesn't matter," The Woman said kindly. "It's just what we like to call him."

My handsomeness having been remarked upon more than once, drinks and food were offered.

"We're having mai tais," Mega Bestseller #1 said, "but we've got fixings for just about anything you could want. Oh, and we've got caviar, lobster . . ."

Ooh, fancy food!

I was feeling pretty thirsty after the long drive, and as soon as my tongue started lolling out, The Woman of course noticed and asked if there was any way to get me a bowl of water. Bikini #1 and Bikini #2 tripped over themselves trying to service me, and what I wound up with was Perrier in a silver bowl. Not exactly what I was used to, but I did feel pampered.

Drinks served, food taken on plates, I closed my eyes and just enjoyed the breeze, figuring we were about to embark on the deeper-conversation portion that human gatherings like these tend to entail in my experience, once the pleasantries have been dispensed with. I wondered what the topics du jour would be: Politics? Philosophy, perhaps? A little Plato, a smidgen of Aristotle . . .

"So," Mega Bestseller #1 asked New Man, "how many weeks for the last book?"

"Twelve," New Man said.

"Respectable, respectable," Mega Bestseller #1 said. "And you?"

"Fourteen," Mega Bestseller #2 said.

"Not bad, not bad," Mega Bestseller #1 said. Dramatic pause. "Twenty-one for mine."

The others raised their glasses in silent salute.

I had no idea what they were talking about, but The Woman, who's smart about so many things, did.

"Earlier in the year," she said, "one of my authors had a book that sat on the *Times*' list for—"

Ohhh. They were talking about the *New York Times* bestseller list. Well, I guessed that wasn't too surprising, given their names.

The Woman didn't get to finish whatever she was going to say, though, because Bikini #1 was saying "I love your hair" and Bikini #2 was asking "Where do you get it done?" And by the time The Woman finished answering, the menfolk had moved on to a different topic involving other numbers.

"What about marketing?" Mega Bestseller #1 said. Not waiting for the others to answer first, he named some astronomical number.

The numbers the others quoted sounded big to me too, but not as big.

"Actually," The Woman said, "the size of the marketing budget is only as good as the things it's spent—"

"I love your bag," Bikini #1 said.

"What kind of wicker is it?" asked Bikini #2.

"I don't know," The Woman said. "I suppose it's wicker wicker."

"You know," New Man said, "she"—gesturing to the wonder that is The Woman—"knows more about publishing than the three of us put together. She certainly is the best editor I ever worked with."

I thought that would do the trick, and that it was right and appropriate for New Man to draw her into the conversation.

But the other two simply looked down into their drinks, embarrassed.

"We heard about what happened to you, of course," Mega Bestseller #1 said to his ice cubes. "Awful, truly awful."

"We read all about it on the Twitters," Mega Bestseller #2 told his ice cubes.

Oh, for dog's sake. Even I knew it wasn't called "the Twitters"—there was no "the" and it wasn't plural.

New Man, to his credit, did keep trying to include her in the conversation, but the others didn't make it easy. I don't think they were being intentionally rude; they just didn't know what to say to an editor who was no longer in the business, a former insider who was now distinctly an outsider.

And so the day continued straight down party lines. I knew there were social situations in which the menfolk talked about important things over their port while the womenfolk were relegated to ladies' topics in the kitchen, real or metaphorical—I'd seen enough episodes of *Downton Abbey* to know that—but I'd never imagined I'd wind up in a gender divide.

And I doubted The Woman had ever pictured her life winding up like that either.

The bikini-clad women asked her a lot of questions about the upcoming wedding in excruciating detail, which she answered with great grace and patience, but by the time that topic was exhausted and the conversation circled back again to what kind of wicker her wicker bag was, she was clearly done.

New Man could see it too. "Perhaps we should go?" he called across.

"Well, we do have that incredibly long ride back," she returned.

We were begged to stay but we demurred. And after more rounds of hugs, handshakes, and air-kisses—with the odd "This has been so great!" and "Can't wait for the wedding!" thrown in for good measure—we were back in the car.

I began to wonder: Was it just me, or did New Man's two friends seem like assholes? Considering how nice he himself was, it was a bit surprising. But then I figured it was a writer thing. Writers spend the majority of their time alone, with fewer opportunities than more normal people for human contact. I knew from The Man that writers have a tendency to cluster with others of their ilk: romance writers with romance writers, literary with literary, and so forth. When it comes to the mega-bestseller category, the pickings must be slim.

But I didn't have a lot of time to contemplate the psychology of why one picks the friends one does, because I was struck by the palpable energy in the air.

"I'm sorry," New Man said immediately.

"It's not your fault," The Woman said. "It's no one's fault. Your friends can't help it if I'm an awkward person to have around right now."

And then they fell silent. No one seemed to know what to say.

As much as I wanted to intervene, to interfere, to attempt to bring a smile out of them, it didn't feel like there was anything I could do. Man. How nice it would be to talk, sometimes.

Chapter Twenty-Five

Back on land . . .

I'd been lounging on the couch after a hard afternoon of eating from my bowl and chasing my tail, and I was contemplating what to do next when The Man burst through the door, looking even more disheveled than usual.

"Gatz, it's been a day and I need a drink," he announced. "Grab your leash and let's hit The Bar."

Since meeting New Woman, it had been months since we'd gone to The Bar. After the era of The Woman ended but before the era of New Woman began, it was the place we'd gone for me to help him pick up chicks; I made one hell of a wingdog. Just like Nick's Italian restaurant was the only place where The Man was comfortable going out to dinner because he could bring me there too, The Bar was his neighborhood watering hole of choice, because . . .

"Gatz!" several people—those playing darts and pinball, shooting pool, or just plain getting drunk—called out upon our entrance. And, as we bellied up to the bar of The Bar, The Man took one stool while I hopped up onto the stool beside him, then The Bartender turned.

"Gatz!" he cried. "It's been way too long! Where you been, buddy?"

I barked enthusiastically. Although I was glad The Man was

doing pretty good in the romance department, I really had missed my tattooed friend.

"The usual?" The Bartender asked.

I barked enthusiastically a second time and he went to get the special bowl he kept just for me, the one with *Gatz* printed on the front. First he tried to blow the accumulation of dust out of it, but then, realizing just how bad the situation was, he cleaned it thoroughly before filling it with clean water. After setting it down in front of me, for good measure, he pulled out a plastic jar filled with doggy treats and placed a couple beside my personalized water dish. Wow, that was a new addition. Like mints on the pillow at a fine hotel. He must've really missed me to have had those waiting for my return.

"And you?" he said to The Man as I wolfed down my two treats, wondering if it was too soon to charmingly beg for more. "What'll it be?"

"A whiskey," The Man said.

The Bartender turned away.

"Actually," The Man shouted, "make it a double—a triple, even!"

"Hey," The Bartender said, "I can fill the whole glass if you want, but you'd be sorry tomorrow."

"Should I?" The Man wondered, looking at me.

I didn't know what to tell him.

"No, no, I'd better not. Just the double will be fine. For now."

When it came, he shot the whole thing back, winced.

Wow, he really had had a day.

"It was awful, Gatz."

I could see that.

"Media training."

He signaled for another double, shot that one back too.

"Media training," he said scornfully again. "Feh. Who comes up with these phrases?"

Don't look at me.

He signaled for a third double and knocked it right back.

"*Training.* What even is that? Like I'm some kind of—"

Don't say it, pal!

Then, for emphasis, I barked loudly to signify my rare displeasure.

". . . person who needs training," he finished lamely.

Right around then, a couple of chicks made their way over to us, taking turns trying to pick him up. This would've never happened in the old days, not without me helping him make the connections. It just goes to show: when you're not looking for action, the action comes looking for you.

The Man had never known how to handle himself when he was interested in a woman, and now I saw that he really didn't know how to handle himself when he wasn't interested in them. Especially half-drunk.

So in order to help extricate him from this awkward situation, I hopped off my stool, trotted halfway to the door, turned, and barked at him.

"Uh, sorry," he slurred to the two women, not really sounding that sorry at all, "looks like I gotta go."

He had his hand on the handle when I heard a voice call after us, "Gatz!"

Turning, I saw The Bartender shaking the plastic thing of doggy treats at us.

"Don't stay away so long next time."

The temptation to run back was overwhelming, but I know when duty calls, and right then, I knew my duty was to get The Man out of there.

Chapter Twenty-Six

After the bar . . .

How does that saying go? Out of the frying pan and into the fire? Yup, that's the one.

"Let's go see her, Gatz!"

Probably not a good idea.

He stumbled out of the kitchen and into the living room, where I was chewing up a storm on the forgotten flannel on the floor. "Let's go see her now, now, now, now!"

Maybe you should call first?

"She thinks media training is such a good idea, such a *GOOD* idea, Gatz!"

I don't think those were her exact words. And shouldn't you wait for a time when you're a little less, uh . . . drunk?

But for once, no one was listening to the sound wisdom of the Gatzer as we made our way, one of us jumping up and down, over to New Woman's place.

Thankfully, she didn't seem to be one of those humans who mind being popped in on unannounced.

"I'm so glad you came!" she said. "I was wondering how it went. Tell me everything!" Then she sniffed the air. "Have you been drinking? Have you been drinking something that isn't beer?"

"'Media training,' they said!" he slurred, whining as he collapsed onto her couch. "'We need to prepare you so you'll be ready for interviews with the media!' they said."

The Man was talking pretty loudly for him, and his volume had roused Hoops the cat, blinking from what looked to me to be his sixteenth nap of the day. Shaking his head briskly to rid himself of the vestiges of sleep, he looked to me in alarm as if to say, *What the hell is going on here?*

For my part, I shook my head as if to say, *Ah, just go with it. Watch the show.*

New Woman sat down next to him, eyebrows raised and already fully wary. "Who is 'they' and who is 'we'?"

"She. The media trainer is a she. And *she* said I need to understand the media process. *She* said I need to refine my messaging. *She* said I need to polish my delivery."

"That doesn't sound too—"

"She said I needed to understand alllllll the different types of media there are and, y'know, that I needed to be all strategic about it and stuff, and understand the various types of interviews that might take place and stuff and allll kinds of *stuff*."

"That still doesn't sound too—"

"She put a camera on me!"

"Wait. What? You mean you were on television today?"

"No! It was for practice. She said I needed to get comfortable with having a camera on me. Here, I'll show you."

He cast about manically searching for a floor lamp.

"That's OK, I can imagine—"

"No, no no, no no, this'll do," he slurred as he found a floor lamp that satisfied his purposes.

He was starting to make me nervous. I was sweating. Her, too.

"OK, now you sit there," he said, indicating a comfy-looking armchair.

She sat down warily, and he took the shade off the lamp so just the naked bulb remained, which he tilted toward her general direction.

"Are you sure you went to the right place?" she wondered. "Because this seems more like a police interrogation."

"And it felt like one." Then, altering his voice slightly, I assumed so he'd sound like a TV interviewer, he began firing questions at her, aggressively yelling things like "What's your novel about?" and "Why did you write this novel?" and "What are you hoping readers will take away from your novel?"

I gotta admit, none of them sounded like particularly difficult questions. None of them were gotcha questions. Rather, they were all the kinds of things he typically got asked when he did author panels. And while he ha-ha-*hated* doing those too, he'd always managed to survive them with what passes for his sanity and dignity pretty much well intact.

But no sooner did she start to answer one of his questions than he'd interrupt, this time using a feminine voice that I assumed was meant to imitate the media trainer, with comments along the lines of "That's not pithy!" and "You need to be more pithy!" and "Why aren't you pithier?"

"Did she really keep harping on pithy and how pithy you are?"

"Yes. Apparently, my 'messaging' isn't 'concise' enough." The Man had set the lamp down on the ground and was now proceeding well down the road to air-quote hell. "My 'messaging' isn't 'thoughtful' enough."

"I suppose I could see how that could get on your nerves."

"Oh, and get this! Apparently, I'm not energetic enough!"

"You seem pretty energetic to me right now."

He threw up his arms. "Well, I wasn't when I was on fake camera! Oh, and I'm also not charismatic enough either. Can you believe *that*?"

Nobody dared to comment on that one. No one was going to touch that one with a ten-foot pole.

"Oh, and another thing!" The Man said. "I almost forgot."

We all waited patiently as he put a fist to his mouth and swallowed, like the whiskey from earlier was thinking about making a rude comeback.

"Smile," he said at last.

"What?"

"Smile, smile, smile!"

"Excuse me?"

"It seemed like every time I said something, the media trainer would tell me, 'Smile' and 'You need to smile more' and 'You look so much better when you smile.' Do you have any idea how annoying it is to get told that?"

"I'm fairly certain that every woman on the face of the planet knows how annoying that is."

"And don't get me started on radio," The Man said with a groan, looking like his drunken-energy balloon had finally been deflated as he collapsed to the floor next to New Woman's feet.

I collapsed by his side. Sometimes all someone needs is a furry companion to lift a mood.

She gently removed his Mets cap, softly ruffled his rumpled hair. If she didn't actually say, "Poor baby," it was definitely in the air. What she said instead was, "They had you practice doing radio interviews too?"

"Yes," he said morosely. "And I sucked at it."

"How can you suck at radio? All you have to do is answer questions you already know the answers to. But nobody will tell you to smile more. No one can see you."

"That's the problem."

"I don't follow."

"Apparently, I talk with my hands more than I thought I did." He lifted his arms, flapped them around a few times. "Apparently, nonverbal forms of communication don't play too well on radio. They don't play on radio at all."

This time she did say it: "Poor baby." Then she added, "But you'll get better at it."

"What if I don't want to get better at it?"

"You'll keep practicing and eventually you'll get better."

"And then what?"

"And then you'll be a success, and I'll be happy for you and jealous of you in just about equal measure." New Woman sighed. "What I wouldn't give for the chance to be as miserable as you are right now. It's every writer's dream."

But The Man wasn't in much of a dream state as he gazed emptily across the room, barely even noticing me next to him, letting his cheek slump against the hard floor.

Chapter Twenty-Seven

The eight days of Hanukkah . . .

'Twas the night before Hanukkah
And all through the house
New Woman had bought a menorah
It was as big as a house

I hate to use the same word twice to create a rhyme, but I got stuck.

Yes, it was the night before Hanukkah, The Man was out on his mission to scout more synagogues, and New Woman had let herself in with the spare key he'd given her.

"What do you think, Gatz?" she asked expectantly, having moved The Man's laptop to the couch to make room for the menorah she'd hefted onto the little table by the window.

Man, that thing is big.

"I know it's a little big, but I like my holidays to be big and festive."

Well, you've certainly mastered the first item. But aren't you at all worried about starting a conflagration?

"You know, maybe I should move it farther away from the drapes."

Phew.

After she readjusted the two-foot-tall item in question, she stood back, studying it.

"Do you think he'll like it? I really want him to like it."

I wasn't sure how he'd take it, but I barked enthusiastically to let her know I liked it. After last year? When the holidays led to The Man and The Woman breaking up? I was more than willing to have someone get the festive ball rolling around here once again.

And I was almost positive we kept a fire extinguisher around here somewhere.

We didn't have to wait long to see how The Man would react, because soon we heard his key in the door.

We both ran to greet him, New Woman throwing her arms around his neck and me jumping at his legs. Then we led him into the room.

"So," she prompted, biting her lip, "what do you think?"

"It's, um, wow, yeah, wow."

"You don't like it?"

"No, I do! I really do. It's, um, yeah, we sure won't have any problem remembering we're celebrating. It's great."

"Oh, I'm so glad!" She threw her arms around his neck again, and he put his arms around her waist while over her shoulder mouthing to me: *Do you know where we keep the fire extinguisher?*

After they broke their clinch, for the first time she noticed the blue crushed-velvet bag he carried in one hand.

"What's that?" she asked.

"It's my tallis bag."

"Your what bag?"

"My tallis bag. For carrying my tallis and my yarmulke."

To illustrate, he zipped open the bag, removed the tallis and yarmulke, draped the former around his neck, and slapped the latter on my head.

I knew I'd end up in a yarmulke.

He spread his arms wide. "Gotta have my tallis and yarmulke on when I'm scouting synagogues."

"Aw, you look so cute. When'd you buy that?"

"I didn't. It was given to me for my bar mitzvah."

"You were bar mitzvahed?" She shook her head. "There's so much I still don't know about you."

You and me both, lady. I thought I knew everything about the guy!

"Ah, it's no big deal," he said, removing the tallis from his shoulders and the yarmulke from my head, and zipping both back up in the handy little bag. "The bar mitzvah, I mean. Everyone seemed to be doing it back then."

"Well, what everyone seems to be doing now is getting ready to make latkes for tomorrow. Who wants to help?"

"We're making latkes?"

"Yes, so I need you to call your mother and tell her we're bringing them. Don't ask her what we can bring, since she'll say nothing like last time, just tell her what we are bringing. Don't give her a choice."

"Did I tell you that my mother's latkes suck?"

"Yes, why do you think we're bringing our own? Call her, please."

Resigned, he left to call his mother. It was a very brief conversation.

"What time does she want us?" New Woman asked, starting to peel potatoes as The Man slowly slunk back into the room.

"One."

"One? But if we're in and out of there as quickly as we were last time, we won't be there for sundown when she lights her candles."

Apparently, New Woman had been doing her Hanukkah research.

The Man shrugged. "We'll just come back and light our own."

Then commenced a fun few hours while we made latkes and didn't talk about parents or religious pasts, and The Man taught New Woman "The Dreidel Song" before she went home to Hoops.

The next day, after New Woman came back, covered dish of latkes in hand, and they were just about ready to leave, I remained in my position on the couch.

"C'mon, Gatz," The Man said, "it's time to go."

Still not moving.

"Don't you want to come with?"

I almost always wanted to come with, but this time . . .

"Ohhhh." The light bulb went on over The Man's head. "I get it. You don't want to eat bad food by yourself in the kitchen?"

Exactly.

"OK, boy. I don't blame you. Hell, I wish I didn't have to—"

"We'll tell you all about it when we get back, Gatz!" New Woman called, tugging him out the door.

I spent the next few hours feeling a mixture of guilt and relief: guilt that I wasn't there to support him through his hours of need, and relief that I didn't have to witness the horrors of The Man with his parents. In fact, I spent so much time envisioning those horrors, guilt tipped the balance.

I should've gone with him. What kind of best friend am I? So what if I had to eat bad food by myself in the kitchen? At least the latkes would be good.

By the time I heard the key in the door signaling their return, I'd worked myself up into a veritable tizzy of worry for him. I went bounding toward the door, intending to greet him with so much love, there'd be no chance for him to spiral further into a mother-induced depression.

But when they came in, they were laughing.

"Oh, Gatz!" The Man struggled to get himself under control. "I know you didn't want to go, but you should've been there."

Clearly.

"Whenever my mother started in with all her usual 'When are you going to write a real book?' nonsense—" He started laughing again, pointed at New Woman. "You tell him."

"I told her that if she wasn't proud to show her friends his books, then maybe it was because she knew in her heart that her friends were simpleminded readers. If they were even readers at all. That maybe her friends didn't know much Shakespeare. Did she know much Shakespeare? Did she know him at all? Because her son's books were brilliant objects of genius, positively overflowing with Shakespearean allusions. No, not illusions. Allusions. And did she not know what an allusion was?"

"She was like a steamroller, Gatz." He demonstrated by whooshing one palm against the other. "Every time my mother made one of her usual passive-aggressive remarks at me—"

"And some of them not so passive," New Woman interjected, "just aggressive."

". . . she'd just steamroller over her again, with these mini-speeches; tirades, really. Honestly, there were times I didn't know what you were talking about."

"I didn't always either, to tell you the truth. I just started talking about Kierkegaard because in my experience, if you mention Kierkegaard, nobody challenges you."

"It was glorious."

So it wasn't horrible?

"It was still horrible," The Man said. "But less than usual. And seeing her take on my mother like that . . ."

"Was I too much?" New Woman said, looking suddenly nervous. "I don't want her to hate me."

"It's hard for anyone to impress her," The Man said. "But she does respect a good comeback. Really, you were perfect. And that stuff about Kierkegaard . . ."

They went into hysterics again.

And you know what else was perfect?

The eight nights of Hanukkah.

New Woman had talked so much in recent weeks about them needing to get each other eight presents that The Man had told her he was beginning to suspect that her real motivation for wanting him to get in touch with his Jewish roots was that she wanted to cash in.

And cash in they both did.

When The Man showed me the eight items he'd bought her, I'd been a bit skeptical, it all being reminiscent of him always buying too many scarves for The Woman, because he hated to shop and was not a terribly imaginative present buyer.

And when he stacked his eight rectangular boxes, all wrapped and the same size, near the menorah, I started getting really worried. What if his idea wasn't as great as he thought it was? I wanted him to do right by New Woman. She'd stood up to his mother. She made him not completely hate spending time with his family. She was a keeper.

But then she ran to get a bag she'd concealed in a closet, and when she began removing items from it, there were eight identical-sized rectangles, just like The Man had got. Only hers were wrapped better.

"Are those what I think they are?" The Man said, a smile spreading across his face.

"Why don't you open one and see," she said with a sly smile. "Just one a night, right?"

"Just one. Now, hmm, I wonder which one I should open first . . ."

"Does it matter?" She laughed.

So they each grabbed the top boxes from their respective stacks and, on the count of three, tore into them at the same time, holding up what they'd received.

He'd given her a flannel shirt. She'd given him a flannel shirt. And there were going to be seven more of each for both.

Not only was his present-giving not the disaster I'd been anticipating; it was a big hit.

"Best. Hanukkah. Ever," he said, taking her in his arms.

After a lot of clinching and kissing, they remembered I was there too—OK, maybe I barked loudly to remind them—and they gave me my Night #1 present too, which was a rubber bone, always an excellent choice.

Then The Man remembered something he'd forgotten, left the room, and returned with a bag containing eight small wrapped items.

"For Hoops," he explained, handing the bag to her. "So he can play Hanukkah and has something to open each night too."

This didn't strike me as being quite fair. Why was Hoops getting Hanukkah presents? He wasn't there. He hadn't helped make the latkes. Was the cat even Jewish?

But when I saw how charmed New Woman was by his thoughtful gesture of inclusion, I set my jealousy aside for the time being.

And, hey, at least there'd been no conflagrations.

Chapter Twenty-Eight

Early Christmas . . .

No, Christmas hadn't gone all Hanukkah by shifting the day around the calendar. But because The Man had told New Woman that I always spent Christmas with his ex, and because New Woman as we've seen likes things to be extra-festive for all, this meant that she wanted to include me in an early celebration. At her place. Having dispensed with Hanukkah for the year, and what a success it was, we were now on to Faux Christmas.

To be honest, I didn't know what to expect from her in terms of decorations, although I suppose that menorah she'd bought us should've given me a clue. Did she favor a real tree or a fake one? If fake, would it look natural and be green or would it be silver? And, if real, what size? Though she'd seemed pretty upbeat the past few weeks, I knew that, like The Man, she suffered from bouts of depression. So maybe it'd be one of those Charlie Brown Christmas trees, all small and twiggy and needleless?

Whoa.

"What do you think, Gatz?" she asked, having let The Man and me in.

Whoa.

It was big, taking up the center of the room, and had no decorations to speak of, save a few bulbs surrounding the upper foot and an angel on top.

"I know it's a bit eccentric." She shrugged. "But at least this way it's Hoops-proofed."

Hoops-proofed?

"The first year I had Hoops, I knew enough not to get tinsel because he'd eat it and that wouldn't be very good for him."

Yeah, cats aren't too bright like that. Dogs are much smarter.

Ah, who was I kidding? I'd eaten plenty of strange things in my day.

"But I thought I was safe with the other decorations, you know?" she went on. "But Hoops just kept knocking all the balls off the lower branches. So, the second year, I just decorated the top two-thirds. That was no good either, though. Because I kept it in that corner over there, like people usually do, but he'd climb up the bookcase beside it and knock off the balls from there. Third year, I didn't put any decorations on it at all, just the angel at the top. So what does Hoops do?"

I wasn't sure how The Man was processing all this, but me, I was breathless with anticipation.

"Hoops leaps at the angel from the top of the bookcase and takes the whole thing down. What a mess! So now what choice do I have? It's either a naked tree in the middle of the room or nothing."

Hoops, man. What a minx. Where was the little guy anyway?

When a little while later New Woman began dishing up her Faux Christmas dinner, with all those great smells wafting through the air, Hoops sure came running then.

After dinner, there was dessert, which included the cookies The Man had thought to bring, now that he's the kind of guy who knows to not show up empty-handed. And after that, there was present opening. The Man and New Woman would exchange theirs on the actual date, but she'd bought something for me, a new rubber bone—classic!—and something for Hoops to open too, so he wouldn't feel left out, even though he'd be getting more on the actual day as well.

Wow, life at New Woman's place sure revolved around Hoops. Imagine, letting a pet take control of things like that?

If this all seems extremely nice and conflict-free, with no tension anywhere, it was. But here's the thing that struck me as weird. The Woman and New Man, for the most part, had enjoyed an almost entirely happy existence together, ever since they'd first met. The Man and New Woman? They had matching neuroses and matching susceptibility to depression, so you'd think everything would be rocky roads and obstacles, and yet here they were, all cookies and blissed-out kissing under the mistletoe. While lately The Woman and New Man had been the ones experiencing uncharacteristic tensions. It made me wonder about The Man and New Woman, watching them open gifts with glee. Was I missing something?

Having dispensed with a happy Faux Christmas, it made me suddenly worry about what Real Christmas would bring.

Chapter Twenty-Nine

Up in the air . . .

The Woman had finally put her elegant foot down about something.

"I don't want to drive out to Indiana to meet your family," she informed New Man.

He was dumbfounded by this pronouncement, and so was I.

"You don't want to meet my parents and my sister before the wedding?"

"No, of course I want to meet them all. I just don't want to *drive* there. It will take nearly twelve hours to get there, and that's only if we're lucky, which we won't be." She ticked off objections on her fingers. "Traffic's never light; it will be worse because it's the holidays; it may be snowing because it's December . . ."

She still had seven fingers to go, but she'd succeeded in making her point.

"So, what are you suggesting?" New Man said. "That we go at some, I don't know, less traffic-burdened time of year, but still before the wedding?"

"Of course not. But do you know that if we fly, it will take less than two hours?"

I'm not sure I'd ever heard New Man groan before, but he let out a whopper of a groan right then.

"You know I hate flying," he said. "It terrifies me."

"So you've said."

In my experience, people saying "What are you suggesting" or "So you've said" is never good, and not something I was used to from these two as a couple.

"But here's something I've become curious about," The Woman said. "The first time I met you, it was in London. You had to have flown there. You can't *drive* to London from here. So how'd you get there if you hate flying? Did you take an ocean liner?"

I hadn't experienced a terribly wide variety of transportation at that point in my life, but even I knew that sounded ridiculous.

"No, of course I didn't take an ocean liner!"

New Man did sound mildly exasperated, but I emphasize the "mildly" part, and anyway, I could tell it was good-humored.

The Woman, in a drawing room-revelation voice, said, "*Aha!* So you did fly!"

That note of suspicion, of doubting what he told her—that was new too. And very disturbing. Perhaps she had too much time on her hands and was starting to overthink things? But what if she began overthinking him?

"Well, of course I flew!"

"But how? Huh? If you hate it so much, how'd you manage it?"

"I took Valium, OK? It's a good thing we didn't meet on my first night there because I was Valiumed up to the eyeballs. I hate that feeling. And while I'm willing to put up with it, when there's no other choice but to fly because it's *for work* . . ."

I could see he was telling the truth. Couldn't she see that? Couldn't she see that the idea of flying genuinely terrified him, so much so that he looked rattled now just thinking about it? I could see his pulse beating quicker in his neck, and I jumped into his lap, nuzzling him. Hey, it sometimes works with The Man when he gets anxious. Which is often.

"Look," he said, patting me on the head, "flying scares me, I know it's not reasonable, but fear isn't reasonable—that's why it's fear—and since it's the only fear I have—"

"It's interesting you should say that," she said, cutting him off, "but that's not really true, is it."

Oh, great. She was questioning him again, like she had reason to be suspicious.

"How is it not true?" New Man asked, beginning to sound wary.

"You say it's your only fear, but when we first met, even though I didn't know it, you'd always been terrified of dogs, so if you can get over that and learn to love Gatz, then I don't see why you can't also—"

"That's it!"

"What's it?"

I'd seen The Man take his own emotional pulse, like, constantly. But I'd never seen anyone physically take their own pulse like New Man was doing now, a smile widening across his face.

He took my face in his hands. "Gatz, if I can get all the proper paperwork, will you be my support dog on a plane? I think with you there, I could get through it OK."

Oh, boy, would I!

"You'd do that for me?" The Woman said, sounding small all of a sudden.

"Of course I would," New Man said, sounding surprised that she wouldn't already know that. "Don't you know by now that I'd do anything for you?"

She looked like she might cry as she came over and joined us on the couch.

"I'm sorry," she said. "I don't know what I was going on and on about."

"It was fine."

"But I must've sounded like such a crazy person to you."

"You've been under a lot of stress . . . anyone would . . ."

A lot of kissing happened then.

Anyway, *that's* how Gatz wound up taking his first plane trip! The Doctor gave New Man a note, the airport said yes to me, and on December 23, we left for Indiana.

I know that emotional support pets on airplanes can be a controversial issue, but believe me when I say that as New Man sat in his first-class seat white-knuckling the armrests, the only thing standing between him and a full-blown panic attack was the Gatzer.

Once we were up in the air, though, he seemed a lot better. I guess takeoffs and landings are the worst. And it seemed to make him more calm still—happy, even—when, the pilot having announced that the plane had achieved altitude and folks could take their seat belts off, The Woman whispered to him, "Do you think if we joined the Mile High Club together, that would help too?"

I thought that was pretty great of her, being willing to make up some ridiculous imaginary club just to calm his nerves.

Then they both disappeared for what felt like a long time, but that was OK. I let the flight attendants pamper me while I looked out the window at all those fluffy clouds. It was all I could do to muster enough restraint not to chase interesting smells up and down the aisle.

Yup, soon I was going to be in *In*-di-a-na.

Chapter Thirty

On the ground . . .

As we deplaned—look at me using all the appropriate aeronautical lingo here!—the flight attendants all thanked me for coming and the pilot said she hoped she'd be working that route when it came time for us to fly back. The pilot even tried to give me a pin depicting wings to commemorate my first flight, but, well, there was nowhere to pin it on me, except my collar, but then The Woman worried the wings would dig into my chin.

New Man took it for me, said they'd start a traveler's scrapbook for me when we got home.

"New York, Connecticut, now Indiana," The Woman said, listing all the places I'd been. "Maybe when we get home," she suggested, "we could get you a US map and stick pins in the places you've been?"

Why not get one of the world, too? Hey, now that I'd discovered the wonders and ease of air travel . . .

In the airport I looked around, craning my neck upward to search for all the tall people. I figured that, given New Man's height, his people would have to be tall too, right?

Wrong.

"Ma!" I heard New Man call, and when I turned to see whom he was calling to, the woman in question was tiny; Lilliputian, even. And the man with her was Lilliputian too. Also, unlike New Man, neither looked particularly urbane. Neither looked even remotely worldly.

New Man bent down to scoop up his mom for a hug, and then he was hugging his dad too.

While he did that, his mom shifted to greet The Woman, holding out both hands, and when The Woman grasped them, his mom asked, "May I hug you?"

"Of course!" The Woman said, bending down nearly as far as New Man had needed to in order to hug her. "It's so lovely to finally meet you in person, Mrs.—"

"No, you call me Ma and him Pa. Oh, and this must be Gatz!"

It was her turn to bend down to me, and when she held her hand out, I placed my paw in it and let her give it a warm shake.

"What a pleasure to meet the amazing Gatz," she said. "I hear it's thanks to you my son can fly now. Who knows? Maybe now he'll finally see the world."

"Ma," New Man said, in the admonitory way kids do when their parents tease them but they don't really mind. He looked around, like he'd been expecting to see someone else. "Where's—"

"Your sister's very busy today; you'll see her later. Now, is everybody ready?"

Just as I'd expected New Man's parents to be—how shall I put it?—not quite so moderately sized, I suppose I'd similarly expected their car to be big and expensive-looking because, well, New Man was so big and expensive-looking, but what they led us out to was something I think is known as a subcompact.

Ma offered to let New Man or The Woman ride up front with Pa, but they both demurred, so the three of us crawled into the back. It was no problem for me but kind of a tight squeeze for the other two, knees to chins and all.

Then we were on our way to Gary, Indiana.

And if New Man's parents were small and their car was small, their house was . . .

Yup, you guessed it: small. It really was just a little brick thing.

I guess Ma was pretty sensitive to what people might think, because before The Woman could say anything—not that she'd do that since she's not at all rude like, well, I can be—Ma whispered, "Every year, he offers to buy us a big house and every year we tell him it's not for children to do for parents, it's for parents to do for children, but still he keeps asking. Maybe you can get him to stop?"

"I'll try," The Woman whispered back. "But maybe if you accepted smaller things from him, like trips, he'd ease off on the other?"

"Oh, we already accept those." Ma waved her hand. "We just don't want him paying a mortgage for us."

After that, Ma took us on a tour of the house, which didn't take long.

"Where's Little Sis?" New Man asked again. "I was sure when she wasn't at the airport, she'd be waiting here to greet us."

"Will you stop?" Ma said. "Your sister has her own place now. You need to stop treating her like a little kid, waiting on your beck and call. She has her own life now. She said she'd be here for Christmas Eve."

New Man looked a bit stung but said nothing more.

Then it was time to eat dinner, which was excellent, and there were TV shows to watch and board games to play. The Woman chose the dog token for me, New Man rolled the dice for me, and I wound up with hotels on Boardwalk and Park Place. Soon I bankrupted everyone else—without even having done anything for myself!—and, after congratulations with high-paws, that was that.

Then Ma let out a yawn that looked pretty fake to me. "You all must be so tired after your long day traveling," she said. She made it sound like we'd driven rather than flown. It'd all been first class too, hardly arduous. "You probably want to hit the hay."

After rounds of "good night" and kisses, New Man and The Woman headed off toward his bedroom, which I'd seen on the tour earlier. It was really small, with a single bed that didn't look like it'd be long enough for him anymore, and the whole room still looked like a kid's room, plus a shrine to all his accomplishments. The Woman had deemed it all "too cute for words."

I moved now to go with them, but Ma called me back. "Gatz, you stay with me for a while, help me with the dishes."

I gave a mental shrug, returned to her side in the kitchen. Sure, I'd hang out for a bit. Then she called out, "Pa! Turn the TV up so I can hear it over the dishwasher!"

Before you know it, we had a veritable racket going there, so loud I could barely hear myself think.

But if the exterior of the house was made of solid brick, the interior walls were paper-thin, which I'd noticed when on the tour earlier in the day, I'd been able to hear Pa cough softly even though we weren't in the same room. Really, you could hear everything from everywhere. But between the blaring TV and the dishwasher and then Ma turning the kitchen radio on too, it was probably only a creature with superior hearing like me who could hear the muffled happy sounds coming from New Man's childhood bed.

Not long after they stopped, Ma turned off the radio and yelled to Pa that "you can turn the TV down now!" and then she patted me on the head, said, "Good Gatz," and told me I could go to bed.

It took me a beat, but then I figured out what Ma was up to: she'd been trying to give The Woman and New Man some mattress time.

Chapter Thirty-One

Christmas Eve morning . . .

If there'd been too much of a racket for me to hear myself think the night before, when I got up the next morning I had plenty of time to think and the quiet to do it in. And what I was thinking, the need to pee notwithstanding, was that things were going pret-TY well; really, a lot better than I'd expected.

It's funny how sometimes you don't even realize you've been emotionally holding your breath until you let your tongue loll and realize: *There. That thing I'd been worried about, that I didn't even know I was so worried about, didn't turn out too bad after all.*

Seeing how The Woman and New Man had been together leading up to the trip—the way she'd started to snipe occasionally, compounded by him not seeming to see what she was going through or, if he saw it, not seeming to know what to do about it—I guess I'd been subconsciously concerned that this trip would be a disaster. That spending time with family, which can be a pressure cooker for a lot of people, was the last thing they needed right now. But the flight had been fab, Ma and Pa were probably the least stress-inducing parents I'd ever come across, and everything was going great.

And you know what was even better?

"I'll take you," New Man whispered to me, having woken up. "Let's let her sleep a bit longer."

Then he went and got one of the special bags he'd packed in their suitcases, and we headed out the door so I could poop and he could scoop.

And, hey! It'd snowed overnight!

It was going to be a white Christmas. Everything was perfect.

Chapter Thirty-Two

Christmas Eve afternoon . . .

Ma had spent the day filling the small house with intoxicating smells. Apparently, one of their traditions was to have filet mignon on Christmas Eve. Do you have any idea how impossible that is to resist? It took all my best-behavior instincts to prevent myself from going into begging mode for the duration.

One person who had no trouble being on their best behavior was The Woman. Once she'd woken up, she did everything she could to make herself useful to Ma: chopping this, keeping an eye on that in the oven, and the like. New Man was very helpful too—setting the table, selecting wines, running out to get last-minute needed items—and I could just see how much he really loved and respected both his parents.

But occasionally he'd wonder aloud about the whereabouts of Little Sis, and as the day drew on, rather than Ma pushing his words aside like she'd done the previous day, she seemed a bit concerned too.

By late afternoon, with no more preparations to be made and the light beginning to fade from the sky, New Man looked to The Woman, his eyebrows raised. "Shall we take Gatz for a walk?"

Knowing it would be cold in Indiana, with possible snow, The Woman had planned ahead and was prepared with waterproof outerwear that managed to be both practical and impeccably stylish.

The snow was incredibly beautiful. Whereas in New York, I was accustomed to city snow—which looks pretty for about five minutes before being destroyed by vehicles and dirt and eight million pairs of feet tromping all over it—this was about eight inches deep of fluffy whiteness, so pretty and so much fun to romp through, leaving little pawprints behind, and so great for:

WHAP!

"Hey!" New Man shouted, putting his hand to the back of his neck and feeling the wet spot where The Woman had nailed him with a perfectly aimed snowball.

"Sorry." She winced a smile.

"Oh, really?"

"Come on. How could I resist?" She bent down and began playing with me in the snow.

Before she could look up, a *WHAP* hit her right on her cheek. She turned to see New Man bending over and hastily assembling another snowball.

"Oh, it's *on*!" she cried, hurling hers at him before he could hurl his at her.

It *was* on, and gloriously so, with snowballs flying through the air, with The Woman and New Man making stacks, hiding behind corners, and ambushing each other with tactical snow-fun maneuvers. And with me racing back and forth in between, offering allegiance to one and then the other, leaping after balls but never being able to catch one in my mouth, jumping on my humans and loving them, occasionally intercepting a snowball with my body via a leap through the air and tumbling into the soft white luxurious ground.

Man, you can't do all that in the city. Well, the loving part you can.

It was into this happy frolicking and mayhem that I heard a car honk and turned to see a small Prius pull into the driveway, which New Man had shoveled earlier in the day.

Then a lanky young woman, nearly as tall as New Man, unfolded herself from the driver's seat, emerging just in time for . . .

WHAP!

"Oh, you did not just . . ." she started to say, reaching down to wipe snow off her coat.

New Man had nailed her in the stomach with a snowball.

There ensued more snowball fighting, but this time between brother and sister, for this was Little Sis, the one we'd been waiting for.

And it was just between them because The Woman had held me back, whispering in my ear, "No, Gatz, let them play for a bit. They haven't seen each other in a long time."

OK, I could understand that, her being sensitive to them needing some sibling alone time. Although it did seem like an odd bonding ritual to me—they hadn't hugged or even said hello yet!

Still, it gave me a good chance to study Little Sis. I didn't know what I'd been expecting. The only picture I'd ever seen of her was the one hanging in the penthouse hallway back home. In that, she was just a little girl. Obviously, if I'd thought about it, I'd have realized she couldn't be a little girl anymore, even though she was about ten years younger than New Man. But I hadn't expected her to be so tall. And I certainly hadn't expected her to seem so, well, angry.

For she did seem angry, from the moment she stepped out of her Prius, and while I suppose some people might get mad if hit with a snowball the minute they step out of their car, in the vigor with which she heaved her snowballs at New Man, there seemed to be, well, more behind it than that.

At last, when the two of them had so thoroughly pelted one another that there wasn't a dry spot left anywhere, they fell into each other's arms for a hug.

"I missed you."

"I missed you too."

When they stopped hugging, Little Sis turned to me with the first look of delight on her face I'd seen. She might have been angry about something, but she was also clearly thrilled to be with her brother again.

"Gatz!" she cried, leaning down to pull me into her arms. "So you're the one who finally cured my brother of his lifelong fear!" She pulled away and held her open palm out. I placed my paw on it for a shake. "Good on ya, Gatz."

As she straightened to a standing position, The Woman greeted her with "Hi! It's so great to meet—" while offering her arms out for a hug.

But instead of stepping into the hug, as humans usually do, Little Sis drew backward and thrust out her palm, kind of like she'd done with me but making it clear she didn't want to be hugged.

"So," Little Sis said, shaking The Woman's hand with the kind of shake I'd only ever seen guys give, meaning hostilely aggressive, "you're the woman who's planning to marry my big brother."

And then she snorted.

She. *Snorted.*

Chapter Thirty-Three

Christmas Eve . . .

Little Sis had grabbed an overnight bag from her Prius, and now we were all back inside the brick house, where Little Sis whipped open the snaps on her snow jacket—*snap, snap, snap, snap, SNAP!*—revealing a white T-shirt underneath, upon which was inscribed in big letters #MeToo.

She angled her body distinctly in The Woman's direction.

"Oh, yes!" said The Woman brightly. "That's such a good—"

"I have snow all over me," said Little Sis, cutting her off and hefting her overnight bag again. "I need a hot shower." She paused long enough to greet and hug her parents before disappearing into the back of the house.

"What was that all about?" The Woman asked, looking stung.

New Man shrugged. "Don't take it personally. She can be standoffish at first."

She hadn't been that way with me!

A few minutes after we heard the shower turn off and the bathroom door open and another door close—because you really could hear just about everything from anywhere in that house—New Man and The Woman went back to take their own showers. They were the first to return, clothes changed for Christmas Eve dinner. Not long after, Little Sis came out too, and it was immediately apparent that she'd exchanged her damp #MeToo T-shirt for an identical dry one.

"I've got plenty more where this came from," she informed The Woman before going to the kitchen to help Ma with the hors d'oeuvres, causing me to picture a dresser with drawers stacked strictly with #MeToo T-shirts.

Hors d'oeuvres, in this instance, consisted of homemade steamed wontons, another family tradition. It took a lot of work—mincing the raw chicken with spices and little green things, rolling them up in little wonton wrappers, and pinching the edges of those wrappers shut before placing them in a steamer basket over boiling water—and The Woman naturally offered to help, but before Ma could graciously accept that help as she had earlier in the day, Little Sis shooed her into the living room with an abrupt, "It's already too crowded in here!"

I hated seeing that stung look on her face again, a previously unfamiliar expression that now seemed to take up permanent residency.

I was about to follow her, I really was, but the smells in that kitchen were too wonderful. And then Pa came into the kitchen, whispered, "Gatz," and then put a finger to his lips in a just-our-secret way before plucking a dumpling off the plate and flipping it in the air for me to catch.

Damn, that was good.

And then the hors d'oeuvres were being consumed and everyone was being called to the table, where wine had been poured and candles had been lit, and grace was said, which was always a nice touch. I don't consider myself to be any one religion, but it never hurts to practice gratitude.

Ma and Pa were at either end of the table, with The Woman next to New Man in the middle and Little Sis across from them. Plates were being passed, and I sat off to the side on my haunches, licking my chops in anticipation. It was New Man who took a slab of the filet mignon and cut it up into bite-sized chunks before setting the plate down in front of me. It wasn't a china plate like I would have been served on if this were the usual Christmas with The Woman's family, just an ordinary one, but with a pleasing holly decoration. But I wasn't complaining about the downgrade. At least they weren't making me eat by myself in the kitchen, and, hey, I was too busy biting those chunks.

In fact, I was so busy with that, I hadn't noticed the rising tension in the air with its telltale no-one-saying-anything tautness.

But then The Woman politely said into the quiet, "Could you please pass the peas?" to which Little Sis responded with a slap on the table, after which she pointed at the slogan on her shirt, demanding of The Woman, "Do you even know what it means?"—and, well, that caught my attention.

"Of course," The Woman said, "that is a very good cause, one I wholeheartedly support—"

"It's not just for women, you know," Little Sis cut her off. "No one in power should ever use their position to exploit someone who is beneath them."

"And I completely agree—" The Woman started to say.

"How can you possibly say that," Little Sis cut her off again, "when you used your position of power over my brother to sexually exploit him?"

"You stop that this instant!" Pa said, in what was, for him, a very admonitory tone.

"This woman is going to be your brother's wife," Ma said. "And it's Christmas. This is no time for that."

From Ma's and Pa's expressions, what Little Sis was talking about wasn't news to them. They knew exactly what she was talking about, had been bracing since her arrival for this attack.

"It's *always* the time to say what's right!" Little Sis insisted. "Social justice doesn't take vacations."

"Look," The Woman said, having recovered some of her poise, "however you might think things happened, it wasn't—"

"Were you or were you not originally his editor?" Little Sis demanded.

"Yes, but—"

"And was a relationship not subsequently begun?"

"Yes, but—"

"I rest my case." Little Sis eased back in her chair and crossed her arms over her chest. "You sexually exploited my brother."

"Little *Sis*!" Now it was Ma's turn to bang the table. "Look at your brother."

We all looked.

"Look at the size of him," Ma went on.

We all looked closer.

"That doesn't matter," Little Sis insisted. "Sexual exploitation has nothing to do with size. It's about power dynamics. In this instance, it's about misuse of power in the workplace."

"Do you know how foolish you sound, accusing someone of—I can't believe I'm going to speak these words on Christmas Eve and at the dinner table—*sexually exploiting* him? No one can sexually exploit him. It's not just that he's too big, to my eyes. He's also too rich! And bestselling! He's a number one bestselling author! How in the world could anyone sexually exploit him?"

"But she—"

"Enough!" Pa had had it too. "She's going to be your sister soon. You must apologize. *Now.*"

"Sorry," Little Sis said grudgingly.

But I don't think anyone was buying it.

Certainly, The Woman wasn't buying it, although, showing incredible poise, she responded, "Please don't say another word. I know that whenever something's important to me, I will fight for what I believe is right."

But if anyone else was buying that, I sure wasn't.

Oh, The Woman made a good show of finishing out the meal and even stayed through dessert, instead of running crying from the room like she probably would've liked to. Nope, she stayed. She praised Ma's cooking and helped with the cleanup.

In fact, she was so good at making it seem like she wasn't really bothered that when once again board games were produced, I half expected her to stay and play.

But she begged off with a fake yawn and a remark of, "I must be suffering from delayed jet lag—but please, you all go ahead," before excusing herself from the room to go to bed.

"Gatz?" New Man called, holding up the Monopoly board. "Are you going to come sit with us while we play?"

I looked from the group in the living room to the hallway leading to New Man's childhood bedroom, where The Woman was, and back again.

"I've got your piece," New Man added, waving the dog token tantalizingly in the air.

Damn, that was tempting. The perfect token. The thrill of watching the dice get rolled for me. The even bigger thrill of winning, without ever actually doing anything. But then I realized: Eh. They'd probably all just let me win the night before.

So I turned tail and trotted after The Woman. Because no matter how much temptation might be waved in my face, I knew where my allegiances lay.

And I knew something else.

The thing that was bothering The Woman most.

For out of all the things that must surely be bothering her right now, and the list was long, the one that stood at the head of the line was:

Why hadn't New Man stood up for her? Why hadn't he said even a single word in her defense?

Chapter Thirty-Four

Christmas Day, very early . . .

The night before, when I'd pawed at the bedroom door and The Woman opened it for me, I'd seen that her eyes were red and there were tearstains on her face. I wondered why I hadn't heard her crying, but when she plopped back down on the bed and put the corner of the pillow in her mouth, I saw why I hadn't heard: aware of the thinness of the walls and sensitive to the feelings of others, she'd muffled the sounds.

So, I did the only thing I could think of to help. I hopped onto the bed and curled up close to her turned back, offering my comfort and warmth. And when, a few hours later, New Man tiptoed in, I remained in that position as he whispered in the dark, "Are you awake?"

I could tell she was, but maybe he couldn't. Normally, at this point, I'd have gotten off the bed so that they could be closer together. I'm not stupid. I know human couples like that sort of thing. But this time, I didn't move. I feigned sleep too and just stayed there, a buffer between them. And when he lay down on the other side of me, I could tell it was a long time before he was able to fall asleep too, like he was troubled. He knew something was wrong. He had to. So at least he wasn't completely oblivious.

The next morning, I listened to The Woman stir beside me while New Man slept on. Then she was up and getting dressed as quietly as possible and grabbing a handy bag to scoop my poop. Before leaving the bedroom, she got the presents she'd brought for everyone out of our suitcases and quietly laid them under the tree before we left, so the others would see them there if they woke before our return.

Outside, there was just a sliver of dawning daylight rising in the distance. I pooped, she scooped, and then, with a heavy sigh, she pulled out her phone.

I thought maybe she'd be texting, you know, stuff like "Merry Christmas!" to her own family and friends.

But after she pushed a few buttons, she held the phone to her ear, and soon I heard a groggy voice saying on the other end, "Hello?" And then, a bit more anxiously: "Is everything OK? Is Gatz OK?"

The Man!

"Everything's fine!" The Woman said brightly. "I just thought, it being Christmas and all, you might want to hear from Gatz."

She held the phone close to me and I could hear The Man say, clear as day, "Merry Christmas, Gatz!"

I barked. Man, I was happy right then, in that moment.

And then New Woman's voice came through, like she was sharing the phone with him, "Merry Christmas, Gatz! We miss you, boy!"

I barked again, really, *really* happy.

The cell phone sure is a fantastic invention.

"Hoops insisted on opening some of his presents last night," she went on, "but there's still a few more to open. We're going to save you some Christmas food for when you come back. Well, it'll probably be bad by then, so we'll just make some more. And—"

A sob.

A really loud sob.

New Woman's muffled voice said something like, "You better take it, and I'll go put some coffee on," and The Woman took the phone back from my ear.

"What is it? What's wrong?" The Man asked.

Now, I gotta say. I love The Man like nobody's business. No one can ever doubt how much I love the guy. But if I had a problem that needed hashing out? He would not be the first call I'd make. It's just that, he has so much trouble figuring out what to do with his own life, it's tough to picture him as being the go-to guy for anyone needing advice. She must've really thought it'd be nice for him and me to hear each other's voices on Christmas Day. But then, once we were on the line and she started crying again . . .

She told him. She told him everything.

And The Man listened. Sure, the guy might not always know what to say. But he's pretty good at shutting up.

But then, once she'd cried and talked, The Man said, "Well. I think you've just got to tell him how you feel."

"I just don't think—"

But before she could finish her thought, from behind us we heard New Man ask: "How long have you two been out here?"

The Woman turned around to face him, said into the phone, "Let me call you back," then disconnected.

"I woke up," New Man said, looking worried, "you weren't there; I looked everywhere. You must be freezing."

She looked over at him, clearly thinking quickly. He noticed her hands. She hadn't put gloves on before coming out. And he moved to take them.

She took a step back.

"Why didn't you defend me?"

Ruh-roh.

"Excuse me?" New Man said.

Wrong answer, pal. This is so not a defensive excuse-me kind of moment.

And then, for the first time, I began to really get scared.

This could escalate. I'd only seen The Woman like this twice before in my life, and on neither occasion, if memory served, had she sounded or looked as bad as this.

"Why didn't you defend me with your sister last night?" she said, biting out the words, really mad now and no longer crying.

"I—"

"Why didn't you defend me at any step of the way? From the first tweet from your stalker to right now?"

Yup, we were definitely escalating here. No longer talking about a single incident, we had immediately leapfrogged to months of pent-up anger and resentment.

If these two weren't careful, they'd ruin everything.

I began to bark at them loudly, begging for them to hear my thoughts. I knew they were meant for each other, and I couldn't imagine my family breaking apart. I didn't want to imagine being in one of those unhappy families with unhappy people. It was too much to bear.

New Man opened his mouth to respond, thought better of what he was going to say, and shut his mouth again.

I barked at him, really loud this time, like, *You better say something, buddy . . . and it better be good!*

"Do you know how hard . . ." New Man started to say, before stopping himself again, his mouth tight-lipped as though forcing the words to stay inside.

Out with it!

"Do you know how hard it is," he began, this time shaking his hand in the air in exasperation before finishing with "to be a man these days?"

NOOOOOOOOOOOOOOOOOOOOO!

Oh, crap. That's not it! Put those words back inside!

"You did not just say that to me," The Woman spat.

New Man groaned at his own idiocy. Me, I felt no pity. When the history of bad opening salvos is written, his is going to rank right up there. I buried my face in the snow.

"I realize how bad that sounded and regretted it as soon as I said it." He groaned again. "But, please, hear me out."

I peeked out to see her cross her arms and tap her boot impatiently against the snow.

"Do you know how hard it was to sit by and watch you getting hurt, knowing you were hurting, and feel powerless to do anything about it?"

"But why couldn't you—"

"Because. It. Wasn't. My. *Place*."

"But you could've—"

"*I* could've? How about *you* could've?"

"Ex-CUSE me?"

Oh, great. Now she was doing that too.

"Yes, you," New Man said. "If you wanted my help, you could've asked me."

"Asked you? Why should I have to ask for help? Why can't you just see I need something and, I don't know, just do the thing I need?"

"Because if I'd just rushed in—like I really wanted to, I might add!—it would've been like I was *interfering*. It would've been like I was . . . mansplaining. Or like I was . . . stealing your thunder or negating your voice. You see, the thing is . . ."

And now he looked so sad. I could see The Woman's face begin to fill with tenderness, just the smallest bit. I slowed my impatient tail wagging.

"That's what I mean about it being hard to be a man—and it came out so horribly." He quickly held his hands up defensively. "And not that it's not harder for women! But I just never know what to do. Like, do I hold the door open . . ."

"You hold the door open," she said with a decisive nod. "If nothing else, you're bigger than me."

"Do I pull your chair out for you . . ."

She shrugged. "I always kind of liked that part."

"And do I fight your battles for you? Because here's the other thing: you are the most brilliant, capable, strongest person I know, and I would never want to do anything to make you feel like I wasn't fully respecting that."

Now it was her turn to open her mouth, stop, and try again.

"I have a question," she finally said.

"Hmm . . ."

"If I weren't a woman or at least not the woman you're planning to marry, if, say, I was a guy friend, and people were attacking me, what would—"

He suddenly turned away and headed for the house.

"Hey!" she called. "We weren't finished!"

He waved a hand over his shoulder, beckoning her to follow. "Come on."

"Where are you going?" she called.

"I'm going to do what I should've done a long time ago," he called back. "I'm going on Twitter."

Chapter Thirty-Five

Christmas Day . . .

We hurried to follow New Man indoors, where we found him in the kitchen. His parents were already there, Ma making coffee and Pa waiting for coffee, and as New Man pressed buttons on his phone, Little Sis walked in, scratching her bedhead and looking groggy.

"Good morning," Little Sis said. "Merry—"

"I love you," New Man said, cutting her off as he glanced up at her briefly, "but I don't want to hear a word out of you right now. Not. One. Word."

Then he went back to pressing buttons like a madman.

The Woman was looking over his shoulder, and I hopped up on a kitchen chair, so I could see too.

When he'd finished, he looked at what he'd written and considered it for a moment. He nodded in satisfaction and then turned the phone around, practically shoving it under the nose of Little Sis.

I watched her eyes dart back and forth as she read what he had typed.

IT'S TIME FOR ME TO MAKE MY FULL CONFESSION! FOR A LONG TIME NOW, I'VE BEEN A COWARD! AND WHEN I WASN'T BUSY BEING THE LOWEST WORM OF A COWARD, I WAS AN ABUSER!

"What the—" Little Sis started to say, before cutting herself off with, "And don't you know you should never—"

But this time, it was New Man who cut her off with a "Didn't I just say not one word?" before turning the phone around and madman typing again.

Even though Little Sis didn't get a chance to finish, I knew exactly what she'd wanted to tell him, because I wanted to tell him too, and my version would've gone something like: *Dude! You've gone ALL CAPS! Not ALL CAPS! Everyone knows that ALL CAPS is strictly the province of politicians who are so pathologically narcissistic, they think people love to hear them shouting, or politicians who are so pathetically insecure they think no one will pay attention to them if they don't shout! Tweet whatever you need to tweet. But, for the love of all that is holy, don't do ALL CAPS!*

But he was in the tweeting zone.

By the time he took a pause to turn around the phone again and jab it at Little Sis, he'd piled up several more tweets:

IT WAS NEVER HER FAULT! IT WAS ALWAYS MY FAULT!

PEOPLE WHO INSIST ON BLAMING HER HAVE GOT THE WRONG END OF THE STICKY WICKET!

I MET A BEAUTIFUL, BRILLIANT WOMAN, AND THEN—NEFARIOUS CAD THAT I AM AND HAVE ALWAYS BEEN!—I USED MY STATUS AS A MEGA-BESTSELLER TO BRING HER UNDER MY CONTROL! BWAH-HA-HA!

Oh, no! He was going on a tweetstorm! Maybe he should, I don't know, pause a bit and read the Twitter room before continuing? What if he tanked his own career doing this?

The Woman started to say as much, but for once, even she

couldn't get through to him. And so, the pattern continued: tweet, turn the phone around so Little Sis could see it, and tweet again.

ACTUALLY, THAT'S NOT WHAT HAPPENED AT ALL. BUT I SUPPOSE IT'S EASIER FOR PEOPLE, SOMETIMES, TO BELIEVE THAT SOMETHING BAD HAPPENED THAN THAT SOMETHING GOOD HAPPENED. AND IT WAS GOOD, SO GOOD, UNTIL ALL OF THIS.

SO, HERE'S HOW IT REALLY WENT. WE MET. SHE WAS SO BRILLIANT, I INSTANTLY WANTED HER TO BECOME MY EDITOR. AND ALMOST JUST AS INSTANTLY, I FELL IN LOVE WITH HER.

I LIKE TO THINK SHE FELL IN LOVE WITH ME JUST AS QUICKLY. I HOPE SHE DID.

REGARDLESS, NO ONE, TO THE BEST OF MY KNOWLEDGE, EVER DID ANYTHING UNETHICAL. IN FACT, AS SOON AS WE REALIZED WE HAD FEELINGS BUT BEFORE WE ACTED ON THOSE FEELINGS, SHE STOPPED BEING MY EDITOR.

SHE EVEN INSISTED THAT SHE INFORM HR AT HER PUBLISHER. I WENT WITH HER. WE HAD THEIR BLESSING, UNTIL, THAT IS, THE TROUBLE STARTED AND THEY, YOU KNOW, WIMPED OUT AND FIRED HER.

A BLAZINGLY COMPETENT EDITOR LOST HER JOB, IN A NUTSHELL, BECAUSE I FELL IN LOVE WITH HER AND SHE FELL IN LOVE WITH ME.

He sighed, and for a moment there, I thought he might be finished. But then, with a deep breath, he jumped back into the fray.

#METOO IS AN IMPORTANT MOVEMENT, EASILY ONE OF THE MOST IMPORTANT MOVEMENTS OF OUR TIMES.

So far, so good. But I was worried. *Please don't say anything negative about #MeToo! That will not end well for you!*

BUT SCOOPING UP THOSE WHO DID NOTHING WRONG ALONG WITH THOSE WHO OBVIOUSLY DID IS, PERHAPS, NOT THE BEST ADVERTISEMENT FOR IT.

Tread carefully, pal!

HISTORICALLY, IN WORKPLACE SITUATIONS, COUNTLESS PEOPLE—OVERWHELMINGLY MALE PEOPLE, I MIGHT ADD—HAVE ABUSED THEIR POSITIONS OF POWER TO TAKE ADVANTAGE OF THOSE WORKING UNDER THEM.

AND IN EVERY ONE OF THOSE INSTANCES, THOSE PEOPLE DESERVE TO BE STRIPPED OF THEIR POWER.

BUT SOMETIMES, I WOULD ALSO ADD, TWO PEOPLE IN THE WORKPLACE FIND "THE ONE." SHOULD THOSE PEOPLE BE PENALIZED, SHOULD THEY HAVE TO MISS OUT ON SPENDING THE REST OF THEIR LIVES WITH THE LOVES OF THEIR LIVES, SIMPLY BECAUSE OF WHERE THEY MET?

DO PEOPLE NOT STILL BELIEVE IN THE CONCEPTS OF "THE ONE" AND "TRUE LOVE"?

I HEREBY ANNOUNCE THAT I WILL DONATE ALL MY ROYALTIES FROM MY FORTHCOMING BOOK TO #METOO, WHICH IS AN INCREDIBLY WORTHY CAUSE AND ONE THAT I BELIEVE IN.

OK, that was pretty good.

BUT I ALSO BELIEVE IN "THE ONE" AND "TRUE LOVE" AND—MOST OF ALL—I BELIEVE IN HER.

SO IF YOU STILL FEEL THE NEED TO BLAME SOMEONE, YOU SHOULDN'T COME FOR HER, YOU SHOULD COME FOR ME. YOU SHOULD COME FOR ME.

And after jabbing that final message in Little Sis's direction and giving her just barely enough time to read it, he turned off his phone.

"And let that," he said, tossing his phone down on the kitchen table, "be the end of that."

"Aren't you going to look to see what people are saying?" Little Sis said. "Don't you want to see how they're reacting?"

"I don't care," New Man said.

"But what about what this could cost you?" The Woman asked.

She didn't have to specify what she meant. No one in that room knew better than her the myriad ways that something perceived as a misstep could cost you.

"I don't care," New Man said again.

She flew at his head.

Reader, that phrase can be encountered in fiction from another century—I'm pretty sure that Jo March did it to Laurie—but it wasn't until I saw it in person for myself that I completely grasped the impact, visual and emotional.

It's like a female is so passionately joyful about something that she physically launches herself at the male, throwing her arms around him and, in her fierceness, practically knocking him off his feet.

And then, having flown at his head, The Woman pressed her lips to New Man's and he pressed his back, and Ma and Pa began clapping, and I began barking, and although I didn't look, because I didn't want to embarrass her, I'm pretty sure I heard Little Sis clapping too.

Chapter Thirty-Six

Christmas Day and beyond . . .

After the joyous flying-at-the-head, a wonderful day was had by all.

Even though it was still really early in the morning, a celebration was declared, Pa pulled out bottles of champagne, and Ma pulled out the orange juice so the drinks could be mimosas, plus she said everyone could always use the Vitamin C.

Then presents were opened. Mostly, I focused on what The Woman had gotten everyone, because she's so good at that sort of thing. As per the uzh, she did not disappoint, each item as thoughtful and lovely as the next. But when it came time for Little Sis to open hers, it immediately became apparent that The Woman had consulted New Man to make sure her present was appropriate and would be appreciated.

Little Sis carefully unwrapped the small box, opened it, and took out the item inside, and just stared at it for a moment. Then she held it up for all to see:

A narrow pewter cuff bracelet upon which SOCIAL JUSTICE WARRIOR was etched across the band.

Little Sis looked at us and we looked back, wondering how she'd react, but then a slow smile spread across her face, followed by laughter, and soon everyone else was laughing.

How well New Man knew his sister. And how well The Woman knew her now too.

And then everyone was giving me presents, making it five presents for the old Gatzer. Each of them had gotten me a new rubber bone, and while some might lament the lack of originality, you can never have too many rubber bones.

More mimosas!

Amazing food!

AND GAMES!

That day, and for the remaining days of our stay, an insane number of Monopoly games were played.

Of course, as Little Sis kept reminding everyone, she was a grown-up now and did have her own life. This meant that, after Christmas Day, she usually had lots of other things to do while we were there that took her away from us during the day, but she always returned at least once a day for a rousing game of Monopoly.

Late afternoon on New Year's Eve, Little Sis came by for a game before heading back to her own place in order to get dressed for some big party. That was when The Woman finally followed Little Sis into the living room alone and got up the nerve to ask what she'd been waiting to ask since we got there.

"Would you be willing to be my maid of honor?"

Little Sis looked completely taken aback. She was so taken aback, in fact, that she didn't respond for several moments. Finally: "I can't believe you'd ask me that."

"I'm sorry," The Woman said, flustered. "I just thought . . . I didn't mean . . ."

"I can't believe you'd ask that," Little Sis said again, "after the horrible way I treated you. Isn't there someone else you'd rather ask?"

The Woman explained then, all about The Blonde, The Redhead, and The Brunette, each of whom would be offended if the other got the better job.

"Plus," The Woman finished, "we're going to be sisters now, and I've always wished I had a sister . . ."

A wide smile grew across the face of Little Sis and she began to jump up and down, screaming, *"YES! OF COURSE!"* and pulling The Woman into a bear hug, which she eased into, laughing.

"But while we're on the subject of sisters," Ma said, walking into the room with Pa close behind, "and big brothers . . ."

Before you knew it, Ma and Pa were telling The Woman all kinds of cute stories about when New Man was a little boy, but they weren't too far into those when Little Sis began to pout.

"I only know all those stories secondhand," Little Sis said. "Ma and Pa had me like other people would get another dog to amuse the first one. Or another cat."

Outraged denials followed from Ma and Pa, but I soon realized this was an old fight with fake outrage all around, after New Man came in to ruffle her hair and say, "But what a cute little kitten you were for me!" and Little Sis broke out laughing.

"Hey, here's something I've been wondering," Little Sis said after we'd all settled around a crackling fire. "What was the fallout after your big tweetstorm?"

"I don't know," New Man said.

"How can you not know? Didn't you check?"

"I told you before." He shrugged. "I don't care."

"And how can you not care? For all you know, you tanked your whole career, and now you'll have to move to, I don't know, a smaller penthouse."

"If it matters so much to you," he said, like any big brother would, "why didn't you check?"

"Because," Little Sis said, rolling her eyes, "I was worried I'd see you'd blown your career." But you could tell she really wanted to know, because: "Oh, fine," she said, rolling her eyes again and pulling out her phone to check.

Scroll.

Scroll, scroll, scroll.

"You're not going to believe this," Little Sis said, holding her phone outward for all to see, similar to how New Man had done to her days ago.

"They *love* him. If anything, they love him more than ever. Look at this! Most people just wanted to know when his next book is coming out. There were a handful of haters, but they got quickly shouted down. Really, it's a ton of love. It's like the fickle Twitterverse just heaved one collective shrug about the whole thing and moved on. How is this fair?" She turned to The Woman. "Only a man could be this lucky."

Not that long ago, this might have been a cue to start the resentment churning in The Woman. It wasn't fair, really, was it? The way one person got vilified and the other got off. It was capricious and arbitrary and didn't make a lick of sense.

The Woman didn't say anything about that, though. Instead, she took the phone and began scrolling the comments for herself.

"Look!" she finally said. "Someone left donation info for that check you promised to #MeToo. And get this. Since you promised to donate, fans have started donating to the cause too in both our names!"

Little Sis immediately pointed at her brother like *You better follow through*, and The Woman added her pointing finger as well, and New Man crossed his heart like *I promise*.

Later, much later, after Little Sis was gone, and Ma and Pa excused themselves to bed early claiming they never managed to stay awake until midnight, we three watched the ball drop together.

Then they swayed to "Auld Lang Syne" and "Theme from New York, New York," and there were New Year's resolutions.

He resolved to always stand up for her whenever she needed him to, and she resolved to tell him if she ever needed him to, instead of making him try to guess.

A bangin' New Year's was had by all.

Chapter Thirty-Seven

New Year's Day . . .

Nothing happened that day. Nothin', I tell ya.

We were all too hungover.

Chapter Thirty-Eight

Up in the air, part II . . .

A lot of people are divided on the subject of vacations. Some people love going, because going means new adventures or relaxation, but hate returning to what they consider to be the daily grind. Other people never want to go in the first place, a lot of type A folks falling into this category, and they can't wait to get back, dreading the whole time they're away.

Me, I think you're doing vacations right if you're happy about it on the day you're supposed to set off and equally happy on the day you're scheduled to go home.

Thankfully, at least on this one, we three were of one mind.

Before taking off, though, it was only natural for The Woman and New Man to check their phones while they still could, in order to see if there was any pressing, suddenly-can't-wait business to attend to.

You know: humans and their phones.

Scroll.

Scroll, scroll, scroll.

"You're going to love this," New Man said, tilting his screen so The Woman could see too. "It's from my old stalker."

"What's she saying?" The Woman asked. "Is she apologizing for all the harm she caused?"

"See for yourself."

The Woman read aloud: "'You are no longer the man I thought you were, if you were ever that man in the first place. So don't expect to hear from me again. There's this bestselling mystery author I've discovered, he's actually a much better writer than you, more handsome too, and—'"

Oh, come on, @SimplySimantha! No one's going to believe that. No one is more handsome than New Man!

The Woman looked at him. "You're being dumped by your stalker?"

"It would appear so," New Man said with a rueful grin. "It's only a shame she didn't dump me sooner. It could've saved us all so much trouble and heartache."

"Indeed. And poor 'bestselling mystery author'! Do you have any idea who she's talking about? Perhaps we should give him a heads-up?"

New Man shrugged. "I'll have to give it a think."

They both went back to their phones.

"Oh, get this," The Woman said after a long moment. "You're going to love this even more."

New Man read it quickly, looked up at her. "This is from your old boss. They want you back."

"I know! Apparently, after your tweetstorm, some of the same people who pestered them to fire me in the first place began pestering them to rehire me."

"Wow."

"Yes, wow." She smiled. "It is surprising, though," she added thoughtfully.

"How so?"

"I'd have thought that, like with front-page stories where there's a deep-in-the-paper retraction at a later date, most people just remember the original supposed offense. You know how it is, when the person's name comes up later, there's a stigma attached to it, with people only remembering, 'I know there's something we're supposed to not like about that person, even if I can't quite recall what that something is . . .'"

"Maybe my tweetstorm was just so good," New Man said with a dazzling smile, "the thing you'd normally expect to happen didn't happen?"

"Maybe," she said, returning her attention to her phone. "Oh, and look at this! Several of the publishers who turned me down when I was job hunting have now written to ask if I'm still available."

"Wow," New Man said again. "So, you've got choices. This is great!"

"Is it, though?" New Woman said, looking thoughtful once again, and a little sad now too.

"How do you mean?"

"You'd think I'd feel vindicated by this, but instead it just makes me sad. It's the principle of the thing. None of them stood by me, none of them wanted me when times were tough. So why should I want them now? I'm not saying I'll never go back to working for a publisher again . . ."

Who could blame her? She'd been badly hurt and it still stung. It would likely sting for a long time.

"But you love editing. You love being an editor. You're not going to cut off your nose to spite your face, are you?"

Oh no, dude! Not a cliché! And you're a writer . . .

"I've missed all that something fierce." Then she smiled. "But what if there were a different way . . ."

I would've loved to hear what she had in mind, but just then the flight attendant came around to our first-class seats and requested they turn their phones off, because it was time for:

Wheels up!

We were going home.

Chapter Thirty-Nine

Later on January 2 and a bit beyond . . .

We took a town car back from the airport—I'm not even sure New Man would know how to use the subway—and during the ride, they told me we'd be stopping first at The Man's place to drop me off. This was totally considerate, plus . . .

Oh boy! Oh boy, oh boy, OH BOY!

After ten days apart, I was finally going to be back with The Man again. Since our first meeting, we'd *never* been apart for this long before!

The driver waited while The Woman and New Man both came to the door with me. And when The Man opened the door following their knock, rather than waiting for the humans to handshake and cheek-kiss like they are wont to do, I lunged at the guy. With me still weighing a trim twenty-two pounds despite all my holiday indulgences, I shouldn't technically ever be able to knock a grown man down. Not unless I catch him really off guard. But, perhaps to humor me and because he had missed me that much too, The Man "let me" knock him to the floor, and once he was down there, I began leaping all over him, licking his face. For his part, he ruffled my fur vigorously and put his face into my neck, hugging me hard.

"Were you a good boy, Gatz?" he asked. "How was your first plane ride?"

Well, of course I was a good boy. And, oh, that plane! To be so high up in the air, soaring through the clouds . . . All the flight attendants loved me; they said they wished all support animals were as well behaved as me . . . I really was good, you know—I even stayed patiently in my seat while The Woman and New Man went off to enroll in something she made up called the Mile High Club!

"I really missed you, boy," The Man said, rising to his feet once I eased up a bit on the licking and he'd had sufficient hugging time for the moment.

"Gatz was *such* a good boy," The Woman said.

"A real rock star everywhere we went," New Man added.

"Gatz!" I heard a different voice call out, the source of that voice being New Woman, now coming to join us from the bedroom.

I wondered why she hadn't come out earlier, as she knelt beside me and, with an "I missed you too, Gatz," began ruffling my fur and I began licking her face. We'd been making quite a racket. She had to have heard us.

It occurred to me that she was being sensitive. She wanted to make sure The Man got his licks in with me first.

Hey, I know that's not how the "get one's licks in first" metaphor is typically used, but I'm allowed to repurpose word usage if I want to. Besides, my licks are *literal* and always a *good* thing.

Then the four humans really were all doing the handshakes and hugs and cheek-kisses things. I must admit that, watching them from the floor, it seemed strange to be seeing these four all together in one place for the first time.

New Woman asked if The Man had offered anyone a drink yet, but The Woman said they were fine and that they needed to be heading out.

Before they left, though, New Woman said she'd seen what happened on Twitter and The Man said how great he thought what New Man did was, and The Woman said she'd been offered her old job back, and other jobs as well.

"That's great!" The Man said, so happy for her.

"That's amazing!" New Woman echoed. "It must've been so hard for you, these past few months, not being able to do the thing you were born to do."

"Yes, it has been," The Woman admitted.

"But now you can have your old job back," The Man said, "or another job of your choosing. This is all so great!"

"You'd think so," The Woman said, "but . . ."

Then she explained all about the principle of the thing and everything else, finishing up with, "So, I was thinking of starting my own freelance editing business."

"That's great too!" The Man said, willing to shift gears to a different reason to be happy on her behalf. "What a good idea!"

"That's what I thought too." The Woman made a discouraged face, like she'd already soured on her own idea. "But driving over, I started looking around online and there are an insane amount of freelance editors out there. You may know who I am, but why would anyone who doesn't pick me over anyone else? It just seems like a lot of noise, maybe too much noise to break through . . ."

Gosh, I hoped she wasn't giving up already.

"I mean, of course I'll give it my best shot," The Woman hastened to add.

She really did sound discouraged, though.

But then it really was time for The Woman and New Man to go, the car had been waiting too long, so after another round of socially proscribed physical contact among the four, the two were on their way.

That's when New Woman turned to The Man, hands on hips, and said:

"Are you thinking what I'm thinking?"

Chapter Forty

A bit more beyond . . .

The answer to that open-ended question, as the days wore on, turned out to be:

Yes and no.

New Woman had been thinking that she should hire The Woman to edit her current work in progress.

"You know how much I've missed having her as my editor," New Woman said, to which The Man agreed.

"You know how much I've hated working with my replacement editor. Or maybe I should say residual editor? Like when you take out a life insurance policy, and you know exactly who you want to benefit in the event of your death. But then you have to put down a residual beneficiary in case the person you really want the money to go to dies first and, I don't know, you forget to change the policy or don't have time to before you die yourself, so then the money will go to at least someone, but it's not who you really want it to go to?"

"I think we may be getting lost in the weeds here," The Man said.

"OK, sure, that too. But what I'm trying to say is that while the editor they put me with after firing her is fine—fine!—or so I keep telling myself, it's not the same; it's not her. You know what I'm saying?"

"I do know what you're saying," The Man said.

"I just love her editing style!" New Woman said. "Maybe some writers can feel comfortable with changing editors, but that's not me. She *gets* me. Before her, I would write first drafts strictly for myself, and then, once I finished that part, I'd begin worrying about the big problem: how to make it something that people other than my mother would want to pay good money for. But you can make yourself crazy with that stuff, like: 'Do I ditch the prologue?' Because some readers hate prologues so much, they claim they don't even bother reading them, which is ridiculous with fiction—it's part of the book!"

You got that right!

"But then I met *her*," New Woman said. "She was my dream editor. She could always see whatever a book needed, and could articulate it with such clarity and kindness, I felt understood."

We were back on familiar ground again.

"It was," New Woman said, "like coming home. And after that, I stopped writing even first drafts just for myself and began writing them with a perfect audience of one in mind."

"Her," The Man said.

"Exactly."

"So, now you want to hire her to edit the book you've been struggling with."

"*Thank* you! Yes. Exactly. That. And I'll be doing both of us—her *and* me—a solid; me, because I'll be ensuring that my book becomes the best it can possibly be; and her, because once we're done, I can give her a ringing endorsement."

"That's a brilliant idea," The Man said, giving her a big hug.

Originally, New Woman had asked if The Man knew what she was thinking and he'd said: yes and no.

Yes, he knew what she was thinking, to the extent that: yes, she could benefit from The Woman's editorial eye; yes, The Woman could benefit from her business as a client.

That was the yes part.

But honestly, that wasn't the problem.

The problem was the no part.

Chapter Forty-One

Still in the beyond . . .

So, yeah, about that no part . . .

"And I'm going to hire her too!" The Man said.

"Wait. What?" New Woman said. "But that makes no sense."

"How can it make no sense? You asked if I was thinking what you were thinking and I said yes."

"I was thinking about me hiring her, and I assumed that's what you were thinking too."

"So?"

Dude, if you can possibly help yourself, stay away from that "So?" It sounds so aggressive, even if the speaker doesn't intend it that way, because it's always open to tonal misunderstanding. That "So?" is where some of the worst arguments start!

"Even if what I was thinking you were thinking wasn't exactly what you were thinking," The Man went on, "isn't it better if we both hire her? Isn't it better if she gets two clients to start her business?"

"But my book actually needs to be edited, while you've finished the edits on yours. You finally buckled down, made the edits your editor suggested. He's happy with the book, you're happy with the book, it's on schedule to be published soon."

"So?"

Dude! Not again! Step away from the "So?"!

"So, what were you thinking?" New Woman wanted to know, crossing her arms over her chest; not a good sign. "That you'll give her a book that there's nothing wrong with and then pay her to look for something wrong with it?"

"Exactly."

"Still not following here." Now New Woman was tapping her right foot; another bad sign. "Won't she see through you, though? When she starts going through the pages with her little red pencil, won't she start suspecting something's fishy when she realizes there's nothing wrong with it?"

He frowned, took a moment to consider the flaw in his plan, then brightened. "Of course she won't suspect! She knows how insecure I can be, especially about my writing—she'll just assume I'm being insecure about my writing!"

"So then you'll, what—write a ringing endorsement of the editing job that can't technically even be called an editing job because no changes will be suggested and therefore none made?"

"*Nooooo*." It was actually kind of obnoxious the way he drew the word out, in kind of a why-isn't-the-brilliance-of-my-plan-immediately-apparent kind of way. "I'll write a one hundred percent truthful endorsement. I'll say that she's a brilliant editor and that people can rely on her judgment to make their work the best it can be. But that unlike some in the profession, she'll never make stuff up just to make stuff up. So people can rely on her to make their work the best it can be, but she can also be relied on to provide reassurance when an insecure writer simply needs to hear: 'You've done what you set out to accomplish. You can put the pen down now. Your book is ready to meet the world.' In short, I'll tell people: she's perfect."

That foot was tapping faster.

Now, I'm no relationship expert, but it seems to me that telling your current girlfriend—the girlfriend you're so into, you even asked her to move in with you a while back—that your ex is "perfect" might not be the way to go. Call her "great," or "exceptional," even. But "perfect"? I mean, I knew The Woman was all that, and I knew from everything she'd said that New Woman regarded The Woman as perfect . . . *as an editor.* But I didn't think she'd relish hearing The Man use that word like that, and I was sure New Woman would respond to this, so I was kind of surprised that what she did come back with was:

"And what will you do if she does find something wrong with your book?"

"Excuse me?"

"I said," New Woman began, and then she repeated what she'd just said, biting off each word separately, which was obnoxious in its own right, before tacking on: "I mean, it's possible, isn't it? That she'll find something you and your editor missed, and then what do you do? Do you go to him and say, 'Um, duh, I know the book is already deep in production, but, um, duh, I think I really need to change the whole ending'?"

"I do not sound like that."

"You absolutely sound like that."

"She's not going to suggest I change the whole ending," The Man said, rather dismissively. "The ending's the best part. I'm sure of it."

"OK, so maybe it'll be something not quite that drastic. But still. If she finds something wrong, what will you do? How will you handle it?"

"Huh," The Man said, stumped. "I hadn't thought about that either." Then he smiled, throwing his arms out wide. "I guess I'll just have to make the changes, then!"

She stared at him.

I stared at him.

Who was this guy?

Outside of my health and well-being, his work was arguably the most consistently important thing to The Man. And now he was cavalierly talking about what to do with it in the event of X, Y, or Z?

He let his arms flop to his sides, but then, closing the distance between them, he gently pried her hands from her upper arms and took those hands in his.

"Look," he said gently, "she's been through a hard time."

The foot began to slow its tapping. Still: "Yes, but—"

"You want to help her," The Man said, "which is so unbelievably generous of you—"

"Yes, well, it would be a help to me too, and—"

"And I just want to help her too. Isn't that what we both want, to do right by someone else who needs it? Shouldn't you want me to do the right thing for someone in need?"

Then he gently cupped her face and kissed her, and she kissed him back, and that right foot was completely still.

But there was something about that foot that still seemed restless to me, and as much as I hoped this was over, I didn't really think it was.

Chapter Forty-Two

Beyond the beyond . . .

You know what's worse than a writer?

Two writers.

Two writers *in a relationship.*

Maybe it wouldn't have been so bad if they were entirely different kinds of writers, like if one were a romance writer and the other a journalist. Sure, with a duo like that, it might be a little *Pride and Prejudice*, at first. But, hey, things worked out fine in the end for Elizabeth Bennet and Mr. Darcy, didn't they?

Two writers who are opposites in some way, in a relationship, *maybe* that could work. So long as an air of mutual respect for the work can be achieved.

But two writers who write *literary* fiction in a *relationship*?

As they might say on *The Sopranos, Madone!*

The egos! Bruised egos! Wounded egos! And occasionally? *Big* egos.

The competition!

I don't know why it hadn't been apparent to me before, during their first several months together. I mean, you'd think I'd have noticed, right? But here's the thing: it hadn't been like that before. It really hadn't. There'd been no competition. But now there was a resource they did feel in competition over:

The Woman.

New Woman would have a session with her and come away from it all blissed out, all "She's so incisive!" and "I can't believe the things she sees that I'm unable to see for myself!"

The Man would try to be happy for her, but then he'd want some of those feelings for himself, so then he'd go see The Woman and then he'd come back feeling all great; smug, even.

"She says the chapters she's gone over so far are perfect," he said.

"Well, of course they are," New Woman said, clearly exasperated with his smug satisfaction. "You gave her a book that was already edited!"

"Still," The Man said, clearly pleased with himself. "It sure is good to hear it."

It went on like that, an escalation of competition for The Woman's editorial attention. Until, one day, New Woman said something to indicate she was concerned that the attention was something more than editorial.

"Here's something I don't get," she said, when he'd returned to the apartment after having been over at The Woman's for something like three hours. "Why does it take so long?"

"Why does what take so long?"

"Editing a book that has nothing wrong with it. How long does it take her to say 'These latest chapters are great' and for you to say 'Awesome' and then to go? For that matter, why can't you just email each other about it or text each other about it? Why do you have to go over there, in person, and spend hours with her?"

It felt as though I'd been waiting for this other shoe to drop for some time now, so I can't say I was caught off guard, but The Man certainly was. How had he not seen this coming? Had no one ever been jealous about him before?

Huh.

"You can't be . . . *jealous*," he said finally, "can you?"

Enjoy it, dude. A woman is jealous over you. Take the win. Take it as a compliment and then, at the first available opportunity, please say something to defuse the situation.

"Can't I?" New Woman said, looking maybe a little embarrassed. "How would you feel if the shoe were on the other foot?"

"But it's not."

"But if it was."

"Well, it's unlikely that the *exact* same shoe would be on the other foot. I mean, do you have any exes who happen to be brilliant editors that I don't know about?"

Doesn't sound like defusing to me.

"No, of course not," New Woman said, twisting her fingers. "It just makes me feel uncomfortable, that's all, you spending so much time with your ex, especially one who happens to be both brilliant and beautiful."

Here's the perfect opportunity. Take her in your arms gently. Validate her feelings. Allay her fears. Tell her that she needn't worry because she's the only one for you.

"Oh, well." The Man shrugged, indifferent.

My head snapped in his direction so quickly, I thought I had whiplash.

Red alert! RED ALERT! Go back! This is not the way!

"Excuse me?" New Woman said.

"We're not married," The Man said, "we're not engaged, we don't even live together."

"That last part is only because—"

"I know," he said calmly. "You won't live with me unless we're married first. Those are your principles. And that's fine. But what about my principles?"

"Your principles?"

"Yes, mine. Am I not allowed to have principles too? And what if mine involve standing by an old friend? Doing whatever it takes to get that old friend back on her feet after going through a hard time? If those are my principles, shouldn't I stick by those?"

"I never said—"

"And another thing."

What other thing? Not another thing!

"I'm thinking of doing a media circuit," The Man said rather arrogantly.

"You're thinking of doing *what*?"

He was thinking of doing *what*?

Talk about your whiplash: Where had *that* "other thing" come from?

Chapter Forty-Three

Beyond the beyond of the beyond . . .

"You know, do some media," The Man stated with awkward aggression, "like a whole circuit of it."

The Man explained that he'd been thinking about calling up his editor and asking him to see if the publicist at his publisher could set up a round of media interviews for him.

"But your new book isn't out yet," New Woman said.

The Man explained that that was the whole point. That with the book already in the can, so to speak—even if The Woman didn't know about that—other than the pretend editing he'd been doing with The Woman, he had too much time on his hands. That he wasn't prepared to start writing a new book yet, so why not use this time to get in some real-life media training?

"Are you sure?" New Woman said. "Why get yourself anxious, doing all that stuff you hate, before you actually have to do it?"

The Man explained that that was the brilliance of his idea. He'd be able to get some practice in before "it actually counts."

This all sounded like a terrible idea to me.

"Can I help?" New Woman offered, once the call had been made and The Editor said that, if The Man was sure, he'd get right on it.

"I don't see how," The Man said.

Ouch.

"I don't know," New Woman said, sounding unsure. "I thought maybe I could quiz you, come up with sample questions you might get faced with."

"Nah, I don't think I need all that," The Man said. "I'm good."

Who *was* this guy?

Well, of course he wasn't good. Of course it turned out to be, if not a total disaster, then a close approximation.

On podcasts and radio, he must've kept forgetting that the audience couldn't see him, because there'd just be these long, awkward silences. And on the one TV show he did, a small local cable program, it might've been better if they couldn't. He gesticulated so widely at one point, he knocked a table over, and he kept losing the thread regarding whatever he'd just been asked. I wish I could've been in the room with him. Watching and listening from home, it was all I could do not to cover my ears with my paws.

After the last not-great event, New Woman tried offering again, more gently this time.

"Maybe before your real round of media events begins, I could try to help you with—"

And that's when he blew up.

"I'm not . . . *malleable*!" he shouted.

Had I ever seen The Man blow up before, about anything?

I'd seen him through the whole spectrum of grays from mildly sad to seriously depressed, and I'd seen him get a little pissed, a little shirty, but I'd never seen him go red before. I'd never seen him *angry*.

So, if I'd never seen it, then New Woman sure hadn't seen it, and neither of us knew what to do with it.

"I don't know what you mean by that," New Woman said, thoroughly confused, "malleable."

"Malleable," he said, impatient, "the capacity to be changed by external forces."

"I know what the word means," New Woman said, now starting to get annoyed herself, "but I don't know what *you* mean by it."

"Malleable, malleable, malleable," he said, putting both hands behind his neck so tight that his elbows banged together in front of his face. "All my life, people have been trying to control me."

"Who's trying to—"

"First you wanted me to see a therapist. Then it was all 'you really should start going to synagogue so my Catholic family will approve of you more.'"

"That's not exactly what I—"

"And then it became, 'Do the media training, why don't you do the media training, you should be grateful for this opportunity other less fortunate authors would kill for.'"

"That's also not exactly what I—"

"When is it going to be *enough*? When am I going to be *enough*? Is that why you named your cat Hoops, because you like making people jump through them? When am I going to have to stop jumping through hoops for you people?"

"I have no idea which 'you people' you're talking about, but I'll tell you what's enough."

She grabbed her jean jacket off the back of a chair and headed for the door.

"Where are you going?" The Man asked.

"Home to Hoops, where I'm appreciated," she stormed, flinging the door open. "I need a break."

How had we all come to this?

"When are you coming back?" The Man asked.

"I don't know if I ever will," she said, slamming the door behind her.

The Man blinked, like he'd just woken up. "What happened?" He sounded so sad in that moment, like a little boy who didn't know what he'd done wrong.

You resorted to all your old self-destructive tendencies and you lost her.

"It'll be fine," The Man said with a dismissive wave of a hand.

Will it?

"She'll be back."

Will she?

He didn't answer. Instead he took off for the bedroom and shut the door behind him before I could even try to trot after him.

And once again, everything felt wrong in our lives, and I was powerless to fix it.

Chapter Forty-Four

Way beyond and way, way beyond . . .

Go after her! If you hurry, you can still catch her! And when you do, apologize! APOLOGIZE!

But he didn't. Loud as I was screaming inside my little brain, he couldn't hear it.

And just like what goes up must surely come back down—unless it, you know, along the way gets stuck on something—The Man quickly went from his self-assured "She'll be back" to a dour "Well, I guess that's that. I've lost her."

He spent a good forty-eight hours—or a bad forty-eight hours, I should more properly say—spiraling ever downward. He didn't eat; he couldn't sleep; he barely left the couch. He was already collecting flannels and empty beer cans on the floor. Before he reached rock bottom, though, it occurred to him:

"Maybe I should apologize . . ."

Thank you!

I was relieved he'd finally gotten there, and kind of impressed that he'd made it there all on his own.

Who knows what would've happened, though, if it had occurred to him to do that right away? Maybe she'd have still been mad; maybe it would've taken her a while to get over it. Or maybe she'd have just said, "Eh. We all have bad days. We all have times we're jerks. Consider it water under the bridge."

OK, probably not that last sentence. New Woman doesn't seem the type to traffic in clichés. But she'd have let it go, maybe, if he apologized right away.

In the event, what happened was: he texted apologies, no reply; he phoned and left messages, no reply.

Was she *ghosting* him?

He was too late.

There was nothing left for me but to conclude that he'd been right when he said, "I've lost her."

We'd lost her.

Well, of course the downward spiral got worse then. Of course it did.

As he lay on the couch in his misery, I decided there was nothing left for it but for me to resort to a tried-and-true tactic: music therapy.

This time, though, I wasn't looking for one particular artist, like when I'd bombarded him with Bruno Mars in the past. Rather, I had a specific theme in mind, one dear to my heart: I was going for happy.

I padded over to the stereo and nosed it on, pawing at the dials until I found something I thought would work: "Happy" by Pharrell Williams. What could be more perfect? It's kind of like the Zen feel of happy-themed songs, like you definitely want to dance to it but in a mellow kind of way. Using my snout, I nosed up the volume because I didn't want it to be too mellow. I was trying to create an atmosphere here.

Then I started running slowly back and forth across the room, but every time I passed by The Man, he just lay there, eyes closed, forearm to forehead.

Ah, thanks for trying, Pharrell. But I guess there are some days where even mental images of you in a Canadian Mountie's hat won't do the trick.

Back to the dial I went. I don't know what it is about me and radio. A lot of people complain there's nothing good to listen to anymore, but it seems to me that, anytime I need a particular kind of tune, it's always been there for me. And this time proved to be no different.

"Shiny Happy People" by R.E.M. was playing! If I'd thought "Happy" was perfect, this was beyond perfect. A whole song about people who are happy . . . and shiny too! Could there *be* a more tail-thumpingly joyous ditty?

Cranking the volume even higher, I started thumping my tail to beat the band.

Tongue hanging out in eagerness, I looked over at The Man to see if the wonderful lyrics as sung by Michael Stipe were having the desired effect.

Nothing.

Sometimes, the only thing a dog can do is go with what he's got. After giving up and powering off the stereo, I began running through the lyrics to "If You're Happy and You Know It" in my head and then barking loud twice in each of the spots where a human would normally clap their hands. I figured that maybe if he got the message about how happy I was, so happy I was barking my fool head off, it would have a contagious effect and my happiness would infect him too.

It wound up adding up to a lot of barking.

Well, at least *that* caught his attention.

"Gatz, what are you trying to do, boy?" He turned to me from his spot on the couch, managing to lean up onto his elbows to see me. "What's with all the barking? Do you not have enough food? Do you not have enough water? Do you need to go for a walk?"

I'd been longing for him to perk up and speak, but now that he had, his voice was so flat and down in the dumps, the happy just went right out of me. I consider myself to be the soul of resilience, most of the time, but if happy can be contagious, the doldrums can be too.

So I ceased my barking and lay down on the floor, head glumly perched on paws, joining him in that sorriest of places: the doldrums.

By the time The Woman came to pick me up so I could go spend a long-overdue few days with her and New Man, that was the condition she found us in.

When she immediately asked him what was wrong, I half expected him to say "Nothing." So I was surprised that he leaped at the opportunity to talk about his problems, going into detail about the fight with New Woman and the fact that he thought they were broken up now but wasn't entirely sure since they hadn't said those words yet but she also hadn't responded to any of his texts or calls.

"So, yeah," he finished. "I've basically given up."

The Woman didn't seem surprised by any of this, and I suspected that perhaps she'd heard it all already from New Woman. She didn't say as much, though, and once he was done talking, she was quiet for a long time, deep in thought.

"You know," she said carefully, "this is kind of what you did with me."

"I don't see that at all." He cut her off quickly.

"Maybe not the details, of course the specifics are different, but you pushed me away. And now it seems you've done the same with her."

"I just didn't want to be . . . *malleable*."

"I don't think you have to worry about that," she said, laughing, but not in an unkind way. "You're pretty much the least malleable person I know."

"What? That's ridiculous. I'm not rigid."

She cocked an eyebrow. He let out a long sigh.

"OK, maybe I can be a little set in my ways, *but* I've been saying yes to her, all the time, so I wouldn't lose her. She wanted me to spend time with my family and get in touch with my Jewish side—I don't even know why you wear a yarmulke!"

Hey, now. Let's not bash the yarmulke.

"Did those things really bother you? Or are you just finding reasons to push away someone else who really cares about you?"

"I even tried *therapy*! God, she may as well have just said—"

"Well, how hard did you try?"

"What do you mean?"

"How hard did you try at therapy?"

"I went once!"

"That's it!" The Woman snapped her fingers.

Light Bulb Moment.

"What's it?"

"You *tried* therapy. You went once to just say you did it. But what if you went again and, maybe instead of doing that thing that some people do—and I'm guessing you did—where you don't really talk about what's real, instead you focus on surface stuff, what if this time you really dug deep and actually did the work?"

"Yeah, I don't think so; that's for people with problems."

"And you have zero problems?"

"That's not what I meant—"

"It would mean a lot to her to know that you really gave it a shot."

He paused for a moment, letting the anger drift out of him and seriously contemplating. "And that would win her back?"

"Well, I don't know about that," she said. "I'm in no position to speak to that. But no matter what happens there, at least maybe you'd know yourself better. At least maybe you'd know enough about yourself to stop sabotaging your own relationships."

He kept his eyes on the floor.

"It would be good for her. But it would be good for you, too."

"I'll give it some thought," he said.

But the way he said it left me with little hope. He'd seemed keen on the idea of giving therapy another go until she wouldn't offer a guarantee that it would win New Woman back.

"I'll give it some thought" my rump.

It's like what kids always complain about concerning adults who say "We'll see"—you can pretty much bet it means no.

He was never going to do it.

Chapter Forty-Five

I'm not even sure what day it is anymore . . .

Once we got to the penthouse, after the angst-filled days with The Man, it took me a while to settle down. At first, I didn't even appreciate the view like I always had before. It was the recognition of that that snapped me out of it. There were a lot of people, not to mention dogs, who would never have the privilege of seeing New York from the vantage I had, and I was a fool not to appreciate that good fortune every chance I got. A fool, I tell you.

With my lifting spirits, I began noticing things: like how great things were between The Woman and New Man again. She was starting to get more clients in her fledgling freelance editing business, about which New Man was massively supportive. Plus, the wedding was fast approaching—!!!—and unlike a lot of couples, who might be experiencing pre-wedding jitters at that stage, sniping at each other about little things and some even threatening to call the whole thing off (not to mention that small percentage that actually do call the whole thing off), these two were having a grand old time.

I looked at them and my overwhelming feeling was one of relief.

Over the last several months, they'd had their ups and downs. There were times, especially over the holidays, when I'd worried they might not make it. But here they were, so clearly in love, better than ever.

Unfortunately, now things appeared to be over for The Man and

New Woman, making me feel like I was playing some romantic relationship version of Whac-A-Mole. No sooner were problems fixed in one of the partnerships than another would pop up in the other partnership, sending that one off the rails.

It seemed like not that many months ago, I was a smug little Gatz, gloating about my two happy families. And just like a great game of Fetch at the park—where I start to think, "Hey! Maybe this will go on forever!"—I'd let myself think it would go on forever, that I would always have happy *families*, plural.

But at least, I thought, looking at The Woman and New Man kiss, I still had the one. It'd have to be enough. So what if it wasn't going to be plural anymore? Like that view I should never take for granted again, I needed to be grateful that even with the one happy family, I was luckier than a lot of dogs.

As for The Man, sad as he was right now and recognizing that he might get sadder still before it started to get better again, it would eventually get better. In the meantime, he'd be licking his wounds, something I'm ideally equipped to deal with, metaphorically *and* literally.

It did strike me as odd, a few days later, when The Woman was due to bring me back to The Man's and he texted her and asked if she could instead bring me to an address he'd provided.

Of course she said yes.

When we got to the address he'd given her, he was waiting outside a building.

"What's in here?" she asked.

"My therapist."

"You—you actually took my advice? Isn't it after hours?"

"I asked for an emergency meeting." He shrugged, looking embarrassed. "You could say I pulled a Tony Soprano."

"And you want to bring Gatz in with you?"

Another shrug. "Hey, if you could bring him to Indiana, I don't see why I can't bring him to therapy."

She smiled softly at that. I find it's moments like this when The Woman is struck with nostalgia and remembers all the reasons she loved The Man in the first place. "Hardly the same thing."

"Maybe not. But I figured that with Gatz with me, I'd feel safer. And if I feel safer, maybe it'll be easier to be honest with her, and with myself."

"Well," she said, shaking off the memories and handing over my leash, "good luck in there."

"Thanks." He smiled softly back at her. She nodded. He nodded. And they went their separate ways.

If the therapist was surprised to see me there, she didn't let on. For my part, I was surprised at how deep her voice was when she spoke—she sounded incredibly like Pamela Adlon—but I didn't let on either. When you get right down to it, wouldn't the world be a better place if *all* therapists sounded like Pamela Adlon?

Once they were seated across from each other in comfortable-looking club chairs, I settled down beside The Man's feet and resisted all impulses to bark as they arose, even when there was an occasional loud sound from the street. I figured my job was to offer support and listen.

The moment he sat down the floodgates opened, and The Man was *talking*.

He talked through his whole childhood and every significant relationship he'd ever had, each of which had failed in the same way: with him self-sabotaging and pushing them away. To say we were there for hours would not be overstating it, and a part of me began to wonder: *Aren't therapy sessions only supposed to last like fifty minutes? What's the bill for this going to look like?*

But The Therapist didn't seem to mind how long it was taking and I didn't either, not even when it occurred to me that I might need to pee sometime soon. Because The Man was finally doing the work. Sometimes he would laugh at himself, sometimes he would avail himself of the tissues in the handy box of Kleenex if a topic made him really sad, but he was being honest about himself. And it struck me as more than wanting to do something big to get New Woman back—he had finally wanted to do this for himself.

While he talked, I kept expecting her to interject with comments or advice on whatever he'd just said, but except for the occasional "And how did that make you feel?" she mostly kept mum.

When he ran out of things to say about the distant past and the recent past, he fell silent.

He waited.

I waited.

Surely this would be the moment she'd say something, tell him what to do.

"You know," he said slowly, "the first time I came to see you, I left with the feeling of, 'Yep, I hate my mother—no news there!' The truth is, though . . . I don't hate her. I happen to know she had a cold mother herself growing up. But having spent my childhood trying to please someone who could never be pleased, no matter what I did, I guess a part of me just gave up. A part of me overgeneralized into thinking all women are that way when, clearly, they're not. So, I get stubborn. I get this idea in my head that I shouldn't be malleable. 'Malleable'—now, there's an annoying word I've used more in the past week or two than I have in my whole life! Now I know how other people feel about the word 'moist'! But that's what it is. I see the way I was as a kid as being malleable, and I don't want to be that way anymore. But I also don't speak up for myself. Considering that I write for a living, I have trouble telling the people in my life how I really feel."

Now he started sounding excited. "But also? I get this idea in my head when I'm in a relationship, like: 'I'm not going to change for you.' Even with necessary compromise, I get tunnel vision about staying exactly the same. This time, though, I did try to change, a bit. But then the old feelings came back and because I'd tried to change a bunch of things, but hadn't said how I really felt about all the changes, resentment built up and then I just, well, blew, I guess."

He paused.

"Could that be it?" he said. "*Maybe*, if I ever get another chance with someone, I should say what I really think and feel? Obviously, I shouldn't say *everything* I think and feel. Even I get that that way relationship madness lies. I mean, heck, look at me right now—if I did this all the time and in every relationship, I'd never shut up! But I should share the important things, and I shouldn't bottle things up because that just takes what are probably solvable problems and turns them into explosive fights that end my relationships. And *maybe* I should recognize that no one is trying to *change* me, no one *can* change me, but there's nothing wrong with someone occasionally expecting me to compromise. So *maybe* I just need to find a way to be more flexible while still being true to myself."

He paused, marveling.

"Wow, you'd think I'd have learned this stuff ages ago. Kinda makes a guy think."

"I think you've made tremendous progress this evening," The Therapist said. "Would you like to make a weekly appointment to come back during regular office hours?"

The Man blew out a breath. "I think I better." Then he bent down, wrapped his arms around my neck, and whispered, "Thanks, Gatz!"

Oh, *man*. Now *I* felt like hittin' the ol' Kleenex box. I *love* being useful!

We walked out onto the street from The Therapist's office that night, and The Man lifted up his hands to his mouth, letting out a "*WOO!*" into the city. I barked along with him, and the night was full of the two of us, letting everything out.

Chapter Forty-Six

Wedding!

Everyone loves a wedding!

Little Sis's long sheath dress was red, The Brunette's was orange, The Blonde's was yellow, The Redhead's was green, and The Woman's three little nieces, who were all going to share flower girl honors, were in short ruffly dresses of blue, indigo, and violet.

Yep, The Woman had gone the Roy G. Biv route on the color scheme. Hey, why settle for just one color when you can have the whole rainbow?

As for The Woman herself—once people had come to do her hair and makeup and her bridal party had helped her into her gown—she was a vision in white. And that veil!

We were all in The Bride's Room, which kind of felt like being backstage on opening night. The Woman and New Man had selected as the site for their wedding a kinda castle in New York State. Present with us were The Woman's Mother, stunning as ever in a silvery gray suit; and New Man's mother, Ma, who hadn't impressed me back in Indiana as the type to go in big for fashion but who was positively rocking a gold suit. She even had one of those fascinator thingies on her head—look out, royal family!

The Woman looked at the clock on the wall. "I can't believe I'm all ready and there's still a half hour until the wedding."

"Well," The Woman's Mother said, beaming as she adjusted the train of The Woman's veil just a smidge, "I did raise you to be punctual."

"Punctual is one thing, but this is ridiculous." The Woman looked a bit nervous as she added, "Maybe I should try to go to the bathroom again first."

Immediately, everyone asked to go with her so they could help. Apparently, that's a thing with weddings: other people holding the bride's dress up for her while she pees.

The Woman, however, put off all offers.

"I think I can manage on my own," she said, grabbing the small handbag that went with the outfit she'd had on before she put on her gown. Partway to the bathroom, she turned her head enough to call over her shoulder, "Gatz?"

No one has to ask me twice. Even if I can't help with the dress-holding part, I love being included in all the behind-the-scenes stuff!

In the bathroom, there were a couple of regular stalls but The Woman went right for the one that had THE BRIDE written on a tasteful sign. It was an extra-large stall, leading me to believe that whoever was running this place, they really knew what they were doing. Brides' dresses require a *lot* of extra room.

Once we were locked in the stall, The Woman immediately hiked up her skirts, pulled a wand-shaped item out of that purse, and proceeded to pee on it.

Huh. Now, *there* was something I'd never seen before.

"Now we wait, Gatz," she said, a trifle anxiously. "It should only take a couple of minutes."

I don't know what we're waiting for, but . . . OK!

While we waited, she wiped off the wand, flushed, and carefully readjusted her dress. There was a handy sink in there too, I guess so brides don't have to wash their hands pre-wedding with the rest of the riffraff, and she availed herself of that convenience.

I'm not that great at gauging the passage of time—waiting for the food to make it from the can into my bowl always seems to take an eternity while a trip to the park goes by in a blink—so being told something will take a couple of minutes? What's that? I mean, hey, it's all relative. But soon, The Woman was looking at a little window thingy on the wand, and then she was waving it at me while excitedly whispering, "Oh my goodness! *Gatz!* We're *pregnant!*"

She bent to hug me, not even caring if some of my fur got on her gown. "Oh, I know you don't know what that means," she said.

Of course I do. My people are a writer and an editor, two writers if you add in New Man, which I do. It'd be three writers if New Woman was still around. So obviously I know what "pregnant" means. It means "meaningful" or "profound," which we definitely are, although I don't know why you'd need a wand to tell you that.

"We're going to have a *baby*!" she whisper-squealed with glee.

Ohhh, *that* kind of pregnant.

Holy mackerel! Wait. We were—

But before I could continue to process, The Woman was whispering to me some more.

"I just couldn't wait any longer to find out. I know I should've told him that I suspected, but we went through this one time before—"

You did?

"And that time we both wound up disappointed. I just couldn't see the point in us being disappointed again right before the wedding. But then I just had to know, you know?"

I'd never seen The Woman dither to any great extent before, but man, she was dithering now. Who could blame her, though? The Woman was pregnant!

"Oh, I wish I could tell him. But it's bad luck for the groom to see the bride before the wedding ceremony." She snapped her fingers with their perfectly rainbow-manicured fingernails. "You should go spend some time with him, Gatz. Oh, I know you have no way to tell him, you don't even know what I'm talking about with all of this—"

I don't know what you're talking about? I felt mildly offended. *After all this time together, do you not know me, lady?*

"Even though he's said he wasn't nervous about today, how could he not be? Could you go spend a few minutes before the wedding with him, Gatz? Having you here with me has helped me out so much, and I know you'd make him feel a little better."

I barked my happy agreement, we exited the bathroom, and The Woman deputized the three little flower girls—Blue, Indigo, and Violet—to take me to New Man.

They giggled as we scrambled our way out of the room, giggled some more as we ran down various hallways until they found a door that said GROOM'S ROOM, and giggled the most when, having knocked on the door and it opening, they saw New Man standing in his tux.

Then they ran away.

"Gatz!" New Man looked very happy to see me. I had the sense of a room filled with masculine energy, and glancing past him, I briefly took in The Woman's brothers, Tall and Short; New Man's friends, Mega Bestseller #1 and Mega Bestseller #2; The Woman's Father; and Pa, New Man's dad.

But it was just the briefest of glances, because in that moment, I only had eyes for New Man, who looked like a million bucks in the most elegant and perfectly fitted tux ever.

And, given his bank account, he could've spent a million bucks on it.

He crouched down next to me to give me a hug, like her, not minding if I got fur on him.

"She knew I'd be feeling a bit nervous right around now," he whispered to me. "She sent you to make it all OK."

You know her so well. And obviously, she knows you well too.

Right then, I wished I could talk. I wished I could tell him the thing that I knew that he didn't know yet. But as good as I've grown over the course of my life at getting my point across—with the occasional, if not entirely reliable, help of the radio—finding a way to tell him he was having a baby was beyond even my advanced skill set. Plus, it wasn't really my place.

So all I could do was lick his face while he ruffled my fur, all the while thinking:

Dude! Just wait until you know what I know!

Chapter Forty-Seven

Ceremony!

Some people, when making out their guest lists for a wedding, invite everyone they can think of: everyone at work; everyone they hope to impress; everyone they think will expect an invitation even if they barely know the person; the mail person.

And while I think that mail carriers don't get invited to *enough* weddings—look at all they do! delivering mail in rain, snow, sleet, and dead of night! and all while dogs like, well, me chase them down the street!—these wedding-list things can get out of hand. The sheer number of guests involved transforms a day that's supposed to be about two people pledging their love into exercises of performative excess.

And sometimes these affairs break the ol' bank, sending the bridal couple and their families into debt. Now, between the wealth of The Woman's family and the even greater wealth of New Man, money was no object. So when they first started planning their big day, they did fall into the kitchen-sink trap of a guest list swelling to ever-greater lengths. And when the size of the list reached four hundred, The Woman had an epiphany:

"Even if we have a reception that lasts five hours," she said, "we'll only be able to spend forty-five seconds with each guest. That's not figuring any time for eating, drinking, dancing, or having a pee. Just forty-five seconds!"

OK, so maybe she'd used a calculator to do the math.

"I don't want a wedding that feels like an assembly line!" The Woman had said. "I want to be able to spend real time with the people we love. I want more than forty-five seconds with each of my parents! I want to be able to have a *pee*!"

The Woman has always been so wise. And New Man, no slouch himself in that department, immediately saw the wisdom in her thinking. So:

Tighter!

Smaller!

Only the people who matter the most!

In practical terms, this meant that, when The Brunette led me into the room where the wedding was to take place—stone walls, stained-glass windows with depictions of great works of art, flowers lining the aisle—the grouping assembled there consisted of the members of the bridal couple's extended families, some of whom would be new to me, but I'd get to know them quickly, and only the very closest of friends.

"Here you go," The Brunette said to The Man, handing me over to him before going off to perform her bridesmaid duties.

Yes, The Woman had invited The Man. Yes, he was one of her essential people. And while some might consider it odd to invite an ex to an intimate wedding, they were friends now. Great friends, who supported each other. Not to mention, who better than The Man to keep me company and occupied during the ceremony and other times during the day when I might need company and occupation?

And, oh my gosh . . .

The Man was wearing a suit! Had I ever seen The Man in a suit before? I mean, there was that one time last year, when he was still trying to win The Woman back. But this suit? It was so much better. It was properly fitted. He was never going to not be a scruffy guy, although he had left his Mets cap home at least, but sitting there in his gray suit, white shirt, and black tie, he looked downright *spiffy*.

"Gatz!"

He and I gave each other the kind of greeting we are wont to do when we've been apart for even a short time, with lots of ruffling my fur on his part and lots of licking his face on my part.

"So," he said, indicating the vacant seat next to his aisle one, "I thought maybe you could sit—"

I settled down on my haunches on the ground next to him, on the aisle side, waiting for the festivities to begin.

"*Or* that could work too," he said. "I guess it would have been hard for you to see over, I don't know, women's hats and stuff. But just don't trip people, OK?"

Would I do that?

"*Or* maybe we could switch? I could move in a seat and you could take—"

I love you to an insane degree and I'm never going to stop—never, I tell ya!—but stop with the seats already! I'm fine where I am. I can see everything from here!

And I was. From there, I could scope out what I assumed to be distant aunts and uncles and assorted relatives I'd never met before because they lived "across the pond," as some call it. *Oh, from across the pond—ooh, fancy people!* And I could see members of New Man's family I'd never met. And couldn't wait to. And I could see the three flower girls—Blue, Indigo, and Violet—giggling as they awaited their cue to enter.

And who was that?

A woman coming in late, edging around the flower girls, tripping over the runner and half losing a high heel before righting herself and readjusting that heel, scanning the room for a place to sit, looking around with that *Which side is the bride's and which the groom's?* look I'd seen others use.

Sure, I'd seen this person in a dress before, once, but that had been a utilitarian dress while this one was va-va-va-VOOM and, oh my goodness, this was:

New Woman!

What was she doing here?

At the commotion, The Man had half turned, and their eyes met in an explosion of mutual awkwardness, and then The Man politely indicated the empty row beside us, but she shook her head just as politely and quickly grabbed a seat in the back row.

Well, of course New Woman would be here. In addition to being The Woman's author, she's her friend. If only it didn't have to be so bloody awkward . . .

But there was no time to dwell on that anymore because now the processional music was starting to play—*ooh, Pachelbel's Canon!*—and people were beginning to process. The whole Roy G. Biv of females, but in reverse color order, ending with Little Sis in her red; all the adult women accompanied by men in tuxes; and the counterpart to the flower girls, a trio of nephews as group ring bearers.

And there was New Man waiting at the front, as all the others processed toward him. He was looking a bit nervous and excited and happy, but far more excited and happy than nervous, as he waited through them all for the one who mattered most, and . . .

There she was!

The Woman! On her father's and mother's arms!

As the whole room gasped at her beauty, it did occur to me to wonder if all this didn't make The Man just a little bit sad, but when I stole my gaze away from her stunning beauty just long enough to check in on him to see how he was doing, I could see that he was OK, more than OK, he was genuinely happy for her, and if that wasn't proof positive that The Woman was right to include him, I don't know what ever could be.

But there was no more time to philosophize because now they were passing by me, and The Woman was winking at me as she passed, leaving me touched that in the midst of all this, she'd spare a wink for good ol' Gatz. Well, of *course* she would!

And then she was actually at the front and the service was about to begin, but suddenly The Woman stood taller, whispering something in New Man's ear, and I'd never seen that guy so shocked he nearly fell off his feet, but he almost did right then. The look on his face! But then happiness jumped firmly on the seesaw, sending shock flying away as he took her in his arms, and even though the kiss isn't supposed to happen until the end of the ceremony, they laid one on each other right then and there.

And while the crowd smiled and laughed at this strange turn in the order of prescribed events, all I could think was that now New Man knew what she knew and what I knew but what nobody else knew yet:

We were having a baby.

Chapter Forty-Eight

Receiving line! Cocktail hour!

Wait. Was I going to have to start calling New Man something else now? I mean, now that they'd gone and gotten married, it wasn't like the guy was exactly *new* anymore.

Nah.

But considering that got me wondering. I'd been called Gatz since The Man adopted me when I was just a few months old. But who had I been before then . . . and what had I been called?

Eh. I'd ponder all that another time, but for now, I was ready for . . .

Par-TAY!

First came the receiving line, with everyone queueing up to hug and kiss the whole wedding party and for the wedding party to greet the guests. I waited patiently with The Man for our turn, noticing New Woman a few places behind us in line. When their eyes accidentally met, The Man gave her a half-hearted little wave and she half-heartedly waved back before they both turned away.

And then it was our turn and the flower girls and ring bearers were all fighting to be the one to hug me first, squeezing me super tight, but I didn't mind. You can't blame little kids for going bonkers over the Gatzer. Happy as I was to greet everyone else, I was the happiest when I reached the end and was embraced by The Woman and New Man. Who cared if her gown got a bit dusty bending over?

Who cared if his tux got more fur on it? It was me! I deserve all the hugs!

Reception line over, it was time to have a cocktail hour while the bride and groom were off having more pictures taken.

I don't do alcohol, but I loved the opportunity to snake in and out of people's legs, getting reacquainted with old friends (Tall and Short were competing to see who could eat more mini eggrolls, a sucker's bet on Tall's part because no one can out-eggroll Short) and making new ones (New Man had this one cousin, man, my sides were going to ache all day from laughing so hard at the jokes that guy could tell—he had a million of 'em, I tell ya!). But I couldn't spend all day glued to the side of Funny Cousin, because I had to move on and mingle some more.

Everyone wanted a piece of me.

And not only did I not have to wait around, hoping people would accidentally drop their pigs in a blanket on the ground so I could snarf them up, but people were actively giving them to me. *They were just giving them to me.*

Every now and then, the eyes of The Man and New Woman would meet across the room and they'd instantly look away. Or they'd be milling around like everyone was doing, circulating, and with backs to each other bump elbows and mumble "Sorry" once they'd seen who they'd bumped before turning away.

Could it be any more awkward?

But now someone was announcing "the bride and groom" and The Woman and New Man were entering the room to great applause, and they were sweeping each other into their arms as they took their first dance: Etta James's "At Last."

Well, you can't beat that.

Chapter Forty-Nine

Reception!

Well, this is awkward.

Dinner had been announced: time for everyone to take their seats. For those who hadn't already done so, it was time to head over to the little table that had these little cards with table assignments on them.

The Man hurried to grab his, then hurried to locate his table, which turned out to be a table for eight, where seven of the seats were already occupied, leaving just one seat vacant beside:

New Woman.

Oh, come *on*, now! What could The Woman have been thinking? She put them at the same *table*?

The Man and New Woman looked all around the table, like people looking for an escape hatch. Except that two people who were looking to avoid each other couldn't very well exit through the same escape hatch, could they? And anyway, what did they think they could do—ask other people to switch? This wasn't middle school. You don't go to a wedding reception and say, "Hey, can you switch seats with me because this person has cooties?"

To their credit, they both must've realized at the same time: *Nope, can't do that.*

Reluctantly, he took the seat. Reluctantly, she said a quick hello to him before turning to talk to the person on her other side.

Damn, it was awkward, the most awkward yet.

And it remained that way through the toasts and the salad course and more toasts, and I'd reached the point where all I could think was, *Just get through the day, kids, just get through the day.*

But then the waitstaff was bringing around main courses, and I was getting ready for The Man to pass some of his prime rib to me under the table, when they both reached at the same time for a wine bottle on the table to refill their respective glasses and their hands bumped and they both said sorry so quickly it was impossible to tell who said it first.

"No," The Man said, "I mean, I'm *really* sorry. I went to see—"

"No, *I'm* the one who should say sorry," New Woman said. "I went back to my therapist—"

At the word *therapist*, my eyes shot over to The Woman, sitting at her cozy table for two with New Man. The Woman had briefly torn her gaze from her groom to note the developments going on at our table, and it occurred to me: The Woman had persuaded The Man to return to therapy; "someone" had obviously persuaded New Woman to do the same thing. And now here they both were. At this wedding. At this same table at this wedding. I squinted at The Woman more closely. Hmm . . .

Maybe you do know what you're doing, lady.

"This time," New Woman said, "I decided to really do the work. And what I discovered was that, yes, I do love my mother too much. And worry about what she thinks too much. The thing is, all my life, I've felt like I had to jump through hoops *for* her love. It's not like I don't get that love from her, I do, but there's always a pretext to everything, like: 'I know you'll pick this college because if you love me you'll want to make me happy and this would make me happy' or 'I don't see why you won't wear this shirt since you know how much I love it for you to wear this shirt,' so I wind up wearing the damn shirt. And I guess that, in my own life, what that's translated to is being like her, adopting her ways. You said I was trying to make you jump through hoops and you weren't wrong. I was doing that! Not on purpose. It wasn't conscious. But I think what I was doing, all along, was essentially saying: 'If you love me, you'll hop through this hoop' and 'Oh, you did that? Well, here's another hoop, now hop through that one.' I was being my mother. And while I love my mother, I don't want to *be* her. Do you know what I'm saying?"

"Completely!" The Man said. "Well, not exactly. Because my situation with my mother is so different. But I completely get the part about therapeutic revelations. Because what *I* learned once I finally started taking therapy seriously . . ."

He proceeded to tell her all about his conversation with his therapist and what he'd discovered about himself.

"Oh my gosh," New Woman said when he was done speaking, "that all makes such perfect sense. I'm really sorry I wasn't listening to you the way you needed me to before. I think I see you more clearly now."

"I think I see you more clearly now too," The Man said. "I want to be better for you. But I want to be better for me too."

Tenderness filled her face. "I'm so glad to hear you say that."

But he didn't pick up on her energy, because his eyes had turned to look down at his feet and I could see the wheels in his brain turning behind them.

"I'm not always going to be happy. And I'm not always going to be fair. Actually, there will probably be a lot more moments when I make myself unhappy, or I try to push you away again. These things take time to work on. I won't be better right away. All I really want right now is to be with you, but I understand if I blew it . . ."

She let out the kindest of laughs and took his chin with her hand, pulling his face to look her in the eye. "I'm not always going to be happy, either. No one is happy all the time. And that's okay.

As long as we're honest and we're working together, and we're treating each other well . . . it's okay."

"Does that mean you'd . . ."

"I want to . . ."

While they'd been talking, The Man had been fiddling with an empty wrapper from a straw someone had left on the table. A paper straw wrapper? At a classy wedding like this? Who let the proletariat in?

But now I saw, as she kissed him and he kissed her back, that his fiddling had shaped the wrapper into something resembling a circle and he was sliding off his chair to the floor, where he got on one knee and—

Red alert. RED ALERT! Douche move! DOUCHE MOVE!

I hurled myself at him and, with all the strength my little body possessed, knocked him to the floor.

He looked up at me, stunned, as I perched on his chest.

Dude, don't be a douche! No matter how good you think this is going, it isn't time to ask her to marry you yet! Only douches ask someone to marry them at other people's weddings. And only the biggest douches do it at their ex's!

The force I'd exerted had knocked the makeshift paper ring he'd fashioned from his hand, and New Woman caught sight of it now on the floor near her feet.

"Oh my gosh," she said. "Were you about to . . ."

He nodded, embarrassed, rising just enough so now he was sitting cross-legged on the floor.

"That would've been a total douche move, to do that at someone else's wedding!" she said, trying not to laugh.

"Obviously," The Man said ruefully. "Apparently," he added, gesturing at me, "someone else could see that too."

At least we were finally all in agreement on this.

"We're not ready," she said. "But ask me again, another day." She reached down, took his face in her hands. "Ask me again when we're both really ready, and, yes, I'll say yes, I will say yes."

Whoa. She knew James Joyce too?

"But right now," she said, "would you like to dance with me?"

He thought about it, and then The Man, who'd only ever been a reluctant dancer at best, said, "Huh. I could dance."

Chapter Fifty

DANCING!

Everyone was hitting the dance floor!

The Woman's Mother and The Woman's Father were dancing. Ma and Pa were dancing. Tall and Short were dancing with their respective spouses. Mega Bestseller #1 and Mega Bestseller #2 had come stag and were dancing with The Blonde and The Brunette—I'd expected The Redhead to bring her longtime girlfriend as a plus-one, but she hadn't, saying they'd broken up. But now she was tapping the shoulder of Funny Cousin, who'd been dancing with Little Sis, and Funny Cousin was relinquishing Little Sis and now she and The Redhead were dancing together, their respective red and green dresses creating a cheery Christmassy combo, and I started thinking. *Hmm* . . . Maybe another romance was in the offing?

They were all slow dancing, The Woman with New Man and The Man with New Woman.

Slow dancing is The Man's specialty, if you can say he has one in the dancing department. But it's not really mine. So I just wove in and out of all the dancing couples, lolling my tongue happily.

But then it was time for line dancing, which wasn't my specialty either, having never been to a wedding before and thus having had no experience of it.

I felt like I was in the middle of the Bollywood-style ending of

Slumdog Millionaire, a film that had turned out in no way, shape, or form to be what I'd been expecting based on the promising title, but had still been quite good nonetheless. The dancing, the romance, the sheer exuberant joy of that culminating moment—that's what we were all exhibiting and feeling now.

I did my best to keep up with all the new-to-me moves. The Macarena! The Electric Slide! The Alley Cat.

And as I did, I thought about relationships and romance. I thought about love.

What is lasting love?

At one point, I would've said it's about things going well all the time, two people never fighting. Happy people being happy all the time. But that's not it. The road will not always be smooth. You're going to hit your share of speed bumps, and sometimes those speed bumps will crop up on you so suddenly and be so high, you'll be in danger of flipping your vehicle over, even if that vehicle is a town car. But when that happens, you've got to hold on to that wheel tightly, with both hands, and just stay the course.

You've got to show up.

You've got to do the work.

You've got to see the other person clearly.

Because in the end, it's not about being in love every second of every day. Who can sustain that impossible ideal?

It's about *choosing*.

So you work through the problems and you choose kindness. You work through the problems as they arise so you can keep choosing to fall in love with that most special person, *over and over again*.

Happiness itself isn't the absence of conflict. It's weathering those conflicts together.

Maybe happiness is hanging in there.

Maybe happiness is choosing to be happy with another.

You love who you love, and if you work hard enough and you're lucky enough, by the grace of the Universe, you get to keep it.

As I looked around me, letting the idea dawn on me that I might soon have two happy families, all I could think was:

I'm a lucky dog.

Then I saw The Man take New Woman's hand as, laughing, the two hurried from the room. I got the sense they were looking to grab some alone time, some just-us-two-people-in-love time. Well, who could blame them?

But then my attention was drawn by what sounded like the music of a million tinkling glasses, and I looked to the center of the dance floor just in time to see New Man place his hands on either side of The Woman's glowing-with-joy face as he lowered his lips to hers, and . . .

Talk about magic!

Talk about romance!

Talk about *love*.

Acknowledgments

Writing and publishing can be a roller coaster at the best of times, so we would both like to thank the following people for making this particular ride a lot less scary and a lot more fun: Pamela Harty, who is not just this book's dedicatee but also a terrific agent and friend, and everyone else at The Knight Agency; Cindy Hwang and Angela Kim—we all know Gatz is very opinionated when it comes to the topic of editors, and he would greatly approve of the two of you; Eileen G. Chetti, for her stellar copyediting; text designer Nancy Resnick, for making our words look spiffy; art designer Sarah Oberrender, for making Gatz look even more beautiful than he appears in our visions of him; managing editor Christine Legon and her whole team, including Hope Ellis and Dasia Payne, and production editor Michelle Kasper and production manager Joi Walker, for a production schedule that kept all the trains running on time; publicist Jessica Brock, for all her efforts on our behalf; Fareeda Bullert, for marketing but also for always so graciously answering all our questions, great and small; and the sales team and everyone else at Penguin Random House, for all the hard work we know about and especially the hard work we never see; and booksellers, librarians, reviewers, and readers everywhere.

Lauren would like to thank: Lauren Catherine, Bob Gulian, Andrea Schicke Hirsch, Greg Logsted, Rob Mayette, and Krissi Petersen Schoonover—it hasn't been the same without seeing all your faces regularly since the pandemic struck, but I am so grateful for your contributions to the Crow's Nest Writers Group over the years; my extended family and friends; my husband, Greg, for life, love, and Jackie; and Jackie, for everything.

Jackie would like to thank: Mom and Dad, for a love and support that could move mountains. To everyone who has supported me on my journey thus far, from my closest friends to my dedicated professors, from kind acquaintances to generous strangers on LinkedIn. Each one of you has had a profound effect on me and the creation of this book. If you think I may be talking about you, I probably am.

Finally, from both of us again: We would like to thank you, whoever you are, holding this book right now. Without you, we're just two women, telling stories to an audience of each other.

Photo by Erin Clarke

Lauren Baratz-Logsted is the author of forty books for adults, teens, and children, including the adult comedic romance *Joint Custody* and its sequel, *The Great Gatz*, both written with her daughter, Jackie Logsted; and the Sisters 8 series for young readers, which she created with her husband, Greg Logsted, and Jackie. Her books have been published in fifteen countries. She has yet to meet a jigsaw puzzle that could defeat her. Lauren lives with her family in Connecticut, where, surprisingly, she has a cat.

Jackie Logsted is a college student studying film, screenwriting, and American studies, training to write and direct movies. She wrote the adult comedic romance *Joint Custody* and its sequel, *The Great Gatz*, with her mother; and with both of her parents, she created the Sisters 8 series for young readers, which has sold more than a quarter of a million copies worldwide. She knows her cat would be jealous to find out she wrote two books about a dog, so she chooses not to tell him. At college, she runs into many dogs and never condescendingly calls them "buddy."